One
City

Alexander
McCall Smith

Ian Rankin

Irvine Welsh

with an introduction by
J. K. Rowling

One City

Foreword by
Rt Hon. Lesley Hinds

Polygon

IN SUPPORT OF THE **ONECITY** TRUST

First published in
Great Britain in 2005 by
Polygon, an imprint of Birlinn Ltd
West Newington House
10 Newington Road
Edinburgh
EH9 1QS

9 8 7 6 5 4 3 2 1

www.birlinn.co.uk

ISBN 10: 1 904598 74 9
ISBN 13: 978 1 904598 74 9

British Library Cataloguing-in-Publication Data
A catalogue record for this book is available on
request from the British Library

Designed by James Hutcheson
in 11/14pt Adobe Bembo
Typeset by Palimpsest Book Production Limited,
Polmont, Stirlingshire

Printed and bound by
Clays Ltd, St Ives plc, Bungay, Suffolk

CONTENTS

FOREWORD

It gives me great pleasure that four of Edinburgh's most famous authors have come together in support of our city. This collection of writing is a project initiated by the contributors themselves in their roles as ambassadors for the OneCity Trust, a charity committed to supporting projects and ideas that will tackle social injustice and inequality in Edinburgh.

Each author has drawn inspiration from Edinburgh in much of their work and each story here, while reflecting their individual writing styles, backgrounds and views of our city, encapsulates the diverse social fabric of Edinburgh. The authors should be commended not only on their contributions of time and work but also on their donation of all royalties from *One City* to the Trust. The funds raised from *One City* will be used to support projects with a literacy or educational theme, apt in a city that has been elected the first UNESCO City of Literature.

In buying this book you are helping to make a real difference in Edinburgh, by making a contribution to the OneCity Trust but also by listening to and sharing the message that Edinburgh should no longer be a divided city but one city with one voice.

With kindest thanks

Rt Hon. Lesley Hinds
LORD PROVOST OF EDINBURGH
PRESIDENT OF THE OneCity Trust *(ex-officio)*

INTRODUCTION

When I arrived in Edinburgh in December 1993, the city was snow-covered, almost dauntingly beautiful and austerely unfamiliar. I did not mean to stay here; I had come to spend Christmas at my sister's and supposed that I would then head south, where most of my friends were at that time.

January came, the snow vanished, but I didn't. Princes Street Gardens were within easy walking distance and entrance to the Museum of Scotland was free; my baby was growing into a toddler and loved tottering around both of them. I stumbled along in her wake, wondering what was going to happen to us, almost as shell-shocked at finding myself in this strange new city as I was to be a single mother, broke and jobless.

It was not Edinburgh's fault that I was in this mess, but as it happened to form the backdrop for the 'rags' part of what might as well be called my Cinderella story, I came to know more about being poor and isolated here than in any other city. It was in Edinburgh, rather than in Paris, London, Manchester or Oporto, all of which I inhabited during my nomadic twenties, that I became most acutely aware of the barriers, invisible and inflexible as bullet-proof glass, that separate those in the affluent and able-bodied mainstream of our society from those who, for whatever reason, live on its fringes.

Most of my pre-Potter Edinburgh days were spent in a small block of flats that housed, at that time, three other single mothers. I was very glad to move in, because it was a big improvement on my previous glorified bed-sit, and in my three years there my daughter learned to walk and talk and I secured my life's ambition: a publishing deal. But it was also there that a group of local boys amused themselves on dull nights by throwing stones at my two year old's bedroom window; there that I wrestled a drunk man back out of my hallway as he tried to force open the front door; there that we were broken into one night while we lay in bed. And I knew that far worse happened to other people, and people not so far away either; my upstairs neighbour used to pause to chat on the stairs wearing sunglasses to hide her black eyes.

Violence, crime and addiction were part of everyday life in that part of Edinburgh. Yet barely ten minutes away by bus was a different world, a world of cashmere and cream teas and the imposing facades of the institutions that make this city the fourth largest financial centre in Europe. I felt in those days as though there was an abyss separating me from those who bustled past me carrying briefcases and Jenners bags – and, in truth, there was.

The OneCity Trust has identified this separation as a '"culture of contentment", which insulates [the more affluent] from the disadvantage experienced by excluded groups and areas'. These groups may include the poor, the disabled, those marginalised due to their ethnicity or, in the words of OneCity, 'people who feel isolated from others and from the benefits of the city', a wholly accurate description of how I felt then.

Social exclusion affects all of us, whether we acknowledge it or not, because it is on the outskirts of society that misery, despair, physical and mental health problems, and the abuse of the self and others flourish. Every city, every citizen, would benefit directly and tangibly from helping bring down those barriers that prevent children reaching their full potential, keep would-be workers from earning and isolate so many within their own homes or their own heads.

The OneCity Trust has enabled both individuals and organisations to make their voices heard, perhaps for the first time ever, within a city and a society that can seem to have forgotten them. The Trust is now analysing that information and making recommendations for a more inclusive Edinburgh, so that changes can be made to make this city more completely ours – *all* of ours.

In the past few years, since the stunningly unexpected change of fortune that hit me with the publication of my first book, Edinburgh has often been described as my 'adopted' home city. True, I retain traces of my West Country accent, and I tend to keep my jumper on even while pale blue men are basting themselves in the watery sunshine in Princes Street Gardens: these are sure pointers to the fact that I wasn't born 'in the old Simpsons'. But as it happens, I have never lived so long anywhere, either as adult or child, as I have lived here. Edinburgh is home now, it is part of me, and I had come to love it long before Harry Potter hit the bookshelves. I am proud to live here, and proud that my home city is committed to becoming a more inclusive place. OneCity seeks to unify: I cannot think of a better goal, for Edinburgh, Scotland or the world.

J. K. Rowling

The
Unfortunate Fate
of Kitty da Silva

ALEXANDER McCALL SMITH

He arrived before the agent did, and was standing there, on the pavement, for fifteen minutes or so before the young man came round the corner. The agent was whistling, which surprised him, because one did not hear people whistling; there was something unexpected, something almost old-fashioned about it. And there was no birdsong, of course, or very little. At home there had always been birdsong, and one took it for granted. Here the mornings seemed silent; the air drained of sound. Thin air. Thin.

'Are you the doctor?' asked the young man, looking at a piece of paper extracted from his pocket. 'You're Dr . . . Dr John. Right?'

He shook his head, and stopped and reminded himself that it was the other way round. In India one shook one's head for yes, which was the opposite of what they did here. It was rather like water going this way round as it drained out of the bath in the southern hemisphere, and that way round in the north, or so people said. Clockwise or anti-clockwise. Widdershins and deasil. Those were wonderful words – widdershins and deasil – and he had written them down in his notebook of fine English words, as he had always done since he was a boy. He had had an uncle who had taught English at a college and had impressed upon him the importance of a wide vocabulary.

'The British left us a very big treasure when they went home from this place,' this uncle had said. 'The greatest language that ever walked the face of the earth. Yes, I am quite happy to say that, even as a patriot. That fine language was left here and you can use it just the same as they can. It is not un-Indian to use English. That nationalist nonsense deprived a whole generation of English. Use it better. Use it better!'

And he had imitated his uncle's habit of writing down interesting words in his notebook. Pejorative, he wrote. Gloaming. Conspicuous.

The young man smiled at him. 'You're Dr John Something, are you?' he said. 'Or are you just Dr Something John? It's not very clear on this paper, you see.'

'I am Dr John,' he said. And he was about to say, 'That is my good name,' because that is what they said at home, but he stopped himself. One did not say good name here; one said surname, which was a strange word, like one of the words in his notebook. Surname.

'Oh,' said the young man. 'I see.'

'Where I come from,' he said, 'in my part of India there are many people called John. It is a name that Christian people use. There are many Johns and Thomases, after St Thomas. They are South Indian names, you see. Kerala.'

'India,' said the young man, and tucked the piece of paper back into his pocket.

He waited for him to say something more, but he did not, but gestured to the door, politely, and told him that the flat was on the second floor and that they should go in and take a look.

'After you,' said the young man. And he went in, into the dark hallway, which had a strange smell to it, like chalk, or stone that has been kept from the sun, like the stone of a cave. He was sensitive to smells – he always had been – and he associated smells with places, with particular corners, with particular times of day. Here, in this country, in this thin air, the smells seemed curiously attenuated. Back home there had been the smell of humanity, and the smell of the sea, of the port, that oily green smell that had wafted up into the town and beyond when the wind was in the right direction. And the smell of coal, and unrefined fuel oil, and the spices from the spice traders, and the rich, sticky smell of filth, just filth. But here there were just faint smells, or no smell at all, just air.

Upstairs, up the winding stone stairway with its iron balustrade and its polished mahogany handrail, he stood outside the dark blue door while the young man fumbled with the keys. And then they were inside, and the young man opened the shutters, that had been closed, and pointed out that from where they stood he might just see the Firth of Forth over the rooftops. There, did he see it? That strip of blue?

The young man smiled. 'People like a view of the sea, you know. So I always try to see if we can see it from a window. It makes them happy.'

He returned the smile. 'I do not like to be on the sea,' he said. 'When the sea gets rough I get very sea-sick. I am not a good sailor.'

'I have never been in a boat,' said the young man, fingering a small blemish on his chin.

As a doctor, he wanted to say to the young man that he should not touch the spot, which could get infected. Fingers were such a source of infection, but most people did not understand that. As a student in Delhi he had remembered peering down his microscope and seeing the colonies of life that the laboratory demonstrator had obtained from a swab taken at random. All those organisms, he had thought, so small and yet so purposeful, so busy with their lives. If he had been a Jain, then what would he have thought? Did they think about the daily slaughter they committed when they washed their hands and sent whole cities, whole dynasties of these invisible organisms swirling down the drain; for them a flood, a biblical scourge.

'Well?' said the young man. 'What do you think?'

'Of course,' he said. 'It is very good. I will take this.'

The young man nodded. 'Good choice.'

They went downstairs together and separated at the front door, after shaking hands. He watched the young man walk down the road. At the corner he turned round and waved.

2

These were the people he worked with. There was the Professor, a tall man with a distracted air about him; the Professor's Senior Lecturer, a woman who said very little, the First Research Fellow and the Second Research Fellow. When he joined them on that first day, they had all assembled in the Professor's room in the university. From the Professor's room they could look out over the top of the trees onto the deserted Infirmary windows, to the wards in which, if the light was right, he could see where the generations of beds had been. He did not like hospitals, which still frightened him, in spite of his having worked in them. He knew that was why he was going to spend his career in laboratories, away from what was happening in the wards and corridors of a hospital; here he was safe, just as an intelligence officer is tucked away from the front line, analysing reports of enemy activity. In the past he had spent time doing exactly that, analysing reports of the enemy, too, staring at the proliferating cells, the cross-sections of the tumours. These were just like the movements of forces across the battle ground; just the same.

The Professor had welcomed him and explained their work. He felt privileged to be part of this group, working at the edge of biology, studying the differentiation of stem cells, trying to tease out the mystery of the chemistry which triggered the growth of human life. The Professor said, 'We're lucky to be doing this, you know. In some places people are hamstrung. They can't do it. We can.' And then he had looked at him and smiled. 'Your people,' he nodded out of the window, in the direction of India, perhaps, 'will doubtless get going on this too.'

He looked at the others, who were watching him. The Second Research Fellow, who was a man of about his own age, wearing a short-sleeved shirt and no tie, was staring at the ceiling while the Professor spoke. At one point he looked at his watch, almost ostentatiously, as if to imply that time was short. He himself would never have dared to do that at home, where professors made or broke careers, sometimes on a whim. Here it seemed different. He had noticed that the First Research Fellow had called the Professor by his first name, which he had even shortened. That would have been unthinkable in Delhi. He had referred to Professor Ghoshal by his first name but never to his face. Never. Not once. It was unthinkable.

He settled into his work. He watched the cells, monitored the medium in which they grew. He looked at them under the microscope and felt what he had always felt, that it was a miracle that he was witnessing; something to do with the breathing in of fire, the transformation of water, the striving of life itself. He thought of the people from whom these cells had come, and wondered about them and the yearnings that had brought this about; the passion, the desire for a child, the resort to the indignities of the fertility clinic. It was love that drove all that, as it drove everything really. We did not want to reproduce that which we don't love. Biology put love into the equation; love made us go to these lengths to perpetuate ourselves. Not that anybody here thought of that, he imagined. These were people of science, who had reduced all this to a matter of cell chemistry and scientific papers. Grants. Money. Intellectual property.

He looked out of the window in front of his desk. It gave out onto a street, a well-ordered street, so clean, it seemed to him, so controlled. There was a pub on the corner that he had ventured into once a few days previously. It smelled of stale smoke and alcohol, and he wondered why people should choose to spend their time in such surroundings. In India one might sit under a tree in a garden, in one of those white plastic chairs and talk to friends. Here you stood inside, with the alcohol, with these pallid people.

3

He was invited to the house of a family from Kerala who had lived in Edinburgh for fifteen years. There was another guest, a student, a tall young man who wanted to talk only of the subject he was studying, something to do with artificial intelligence. The oldest son of the house, who was four years or so younger than he was, in his mid-twenties, showed him the car that he had just bought and which was parked out in the street. He was inordinately proud of it, and he showed him its special features. He could not help but smile; he had no interest in cars, but for this young man the car was proof in metal of what he had achieved. He was on the way to becoming a chartered accountant.

'You can do well in this country,' the young man said, touching the highly polished bodywork of the car, 'if you let your own people help you. Generally we keep to ourselves. Some people don't, of course. But I think it's safer that way.'

'Safer?'

'You can get yourself beaten up,' he said, rubbing at an imaginary scratch on the car door. 'Or just put down, and sometimes there's not much difference. Don't be fooled by the rhetoric. And Scotland is as bad as anywhere else. They like to think that they're different from the rest of the country, but . . .'

He felt uneasy. He did not think it good manners to discuss people in this way. This was their country, after all, just as India was his. He would not have taken well to a Scotsman in India discussing the faults of the Indians. It was a question of courtesy, he thought.

'But they aren't tolerant?'

The young man smiled. 'On the surface. And sometimes more than that. It's . . . well, it's complex. The only way is to find out. You'll find out.'

4

He went into an Episcopalian Church, on impulse, because he was walking past the church and he saw that the service was about to begin. He had been brought up in the Church of South India, which was Anglican, and he knew that this was the local equivalent. He sat at the back, a row or two away from the rest of the small congregation. An elderly woman turned round and smiled at him, and he nodded to her in return. Then he studied the liturgy, and saw the familiar words which he had learned in his youth and which gave him a curious sense of belonging.

He had lost his faith early. He remembered the day it had happened, when he was sixteen, and when the teacher in charge of religious instruction at school had spoken of the omnipotence of God. He had looked at the boy sitting next to him and had nudged him: 'But if God can do anything, then why does he allow suffering? Why does he allow the wicked to get away with it?'

The other boy had raised a finger to his lips, to silence him. But he had persisted, and the boy had eventually whispered, 'Don't you know? It's all lies. Everything they're teaching us in this place is lies. It's as much invention as the Hindu gods. Ganesh and all the rest. Just pretend to believe the lies until you're out of here and then you can stop.'

He had pretended to believe but that was all. And he knew, later on, when he stood at the dissecting table in medical school and stared down at the body stretched out before him, the body of a street hawker, he suspected, or an indentured labourer, a body marked by labour and hardship; he knew then that he had made the right decision. Because there could not be an omnipotent God and all this suffering. It did not make sense, and it gave him no comfort. If one was looking for comfort in this life, then it would have been better, he thought, to seek comfort in the prospect that something might be done about the suffering. Yet here he was in this church, out of sheer loneliness, pretending to believe. He looked at the familiar symbol, the cross. It said nothing to him now, in a religious sense; of course it was much more than that: it was a symbol of his particular people, for him a symbol of enlightenment in the face of all those Hindu gods and rituals. And yet it had always seemed to him to be such a cruel symbol – an instrument of execution, after all.

How much better would Ganesh have been, with his benign expression and his elephantine understanding, and his one hundred and forty names.

He sat through the service, and thought about home. There was no cure for home-sickness – none. All that one could do was wait for it to subside, which he knew it would. He had felt home-sick in Delhi, in the first year of his medical course, when he had lived in a rowdy student hostel noted for its greasy food and loud music. My problem is loneliness, he thought. I need family life. I need to have somewhere to go back to, some place, where everything is familiar.

After the service, a woman came up to him and touched his sleeve. 'You must join us for coffee,' she said. 'Downstairs. You'll be very welcome.'

He was about to decline, when she said, 'Are you from South India?'

He was touched that she knew. Some of the people in the lab had assumed that he was Muslim – which showed how much they knew about the world. But this woman, with her earnest invitation, knew.

'Yes,' he said. 'Cochi.' He used the new name, but corrected himself; she might not know. And people still said Bombay, everywhere. 'Cochin.'

'Ah, Cochi,' she said. 'We had somebody from there a few years ago. One of their bishops, I think. Such a colourful robe, as I remember.'

She led him down some stairs and into a hall where people were clustering around a trestle table on which a tea urn had been placed. As they served him his cup of tea, he wondered what the young accountant, the one with the high-powered car, would have thought of this scene. He would have laughed, no doubt, to see him at what was effectively a church social. And yet, he thought, why should people laugh at other people who are just trying to be kind?

He stood with his cup of tea, talking to the woman who had invited him. Then suddenly she was distracted and he found himself alone. He glanced about him. He need not stay more than a few minutes – that would be enough to be polite. Then he could go back to his flat and wait there until it was evening and he could go and see a film somewhere or have a meal in a restaurant if he felt like splashing out.

On the way back from the church, he stopped for a cup of coffee in a coffee bar at the end of his street. As he stood at a high table, self-consciously blowing on his coffee to cool it, a young woman – she must have been a couple of years younger than him, or perhaps even his age – asked if he was reading the paper on his table. He handed it to her. She said, 'You live in the flat above mine, don't you? I've seen you.'

He had not seen her. He had only seen one neighbour so far, a middle-aged man who lived with a younger woman on the ground floor.

She reached out to shake his hand. 'One should get to know one's neighbours,' she said, smiling. 'You never know when you're going to want to borrow something from them.'

'I am happy for you to borrow from me,' he said. 'Any time.' But then he thought: I have virtually nothing in the flat, and smiled. 'Not that I have anything to lend you. I mean, I have no food in the flat. No sugar or milk or the things that people like to borrow.'

She laughed at the admission. 'Then you must come and have a meal with me, in my place. Why don't you?'

He hesitated. He had been warned that people said things that they didn't mean in this country; he had been told that an invitation did not necessarily mean that you were invited. It was just one of the ways in which people were polite. Was this such an invitation, or was he really being invited?

'When?' he asked. He had blurted out the question without thinking. Now, if the invitation was not a real invitation, he would have embarrassed her. She could hardly say: never.

'Tonight,' she said. 'If you've got nothing better to do. Come tonight.'

He accepted, and they agreed that he would come downstairs at seven-thirty. Again he remembered that times were not always meant. Seven-thirty might mean a quarter to eight, or even eight o'clock. He wanted to ask, but felt too embarrassed to do so. So he nodded, remembering to shake his head the right way for this country, to say no when he meant yes.

5

She was called Jennifer, but told him to call her Jen, as everybody did. 'Nobody calls me Jennifer anymore, apart from my mother. Mothers stick to your real names, don't they, even when the whole world calls you something else.'

She worked for a large insurance company, and had done so for two years, after leaving university. She had let out a room in the flat for a year after she had bought it, but had grown tired of her tenant, who smoked and never cleared up in the kitchen. 'It was the hardest thing I ever had to do,' she said. 'I had to ask her to leave, and she looked at me like this – with great reproachful eyes – and asked me whether I had felt that way about her all the time. "It's hard to think that you've been sharing with somebody who hates you" she said. Those were her words. It was awful.'

He told her about the flat that he had lived in in Delhi, as a doctor. It was next door to a Punjabi transvestite who would sit on his balcony and sing Bollywood love songs. 'He sang the woman's part in his falsetto voice and then lowered it to sing the man's part. But his heart was in the woman's part. You could tell.'

She laughed. 'I can just see it,' she said.

He asked her whether she knew India. 'I've been there once,' she said. 'I went to Thailand with a friend and we stopped for five days in Bombay on the way. We didn't know what to do. There was this vast city around us and we didn't really know how to get out of it.'

'I wouldn't like to be trapped in Bombay,' he said.

It seemed to him that she was hesitating over her next remark, as if she was wondering whether she could tell him what she thought of India. That was it. Nobody liked to tell you what they really thought, but he knew.

'You can tell me what you really thought,' he said. 'You were shocked by India, weren't you?'

She took a sip from her wine glass. They were sitting in her living room before going into the kitchen for dinner. 'Yes,' she said. 'I was shocked.'

'Tell me,' he said.

'Well, I couldn't get over the sheer poverty of so many of the people. Not just a few of the people. Millions and millions of them. People with nothing. People who lived in little shelters beside the road or on the edge of railway stations, with a few rags hanging from poles at the sides, and heaps of fetid rubbish and dogs crawling over the litter.'

'You would not see that in the south,' he said, and added, quickly, 'but I know what you mean. We Indians tend not to see it. Or we see it and it doesn't register with us as anything exceptional, because we have always seen it. We have seen these poor people and they're always there, like trees, or rocks, or clouds in the sky. Just part of the scenery.'

He watched her while he spoke. It was difficult to explain to people who did not understand, who thought that everywhere should be the same as their little part of the world. It was difficult to understand that things were just different because they were, because there was a very different history.

'Just part of the scenery?'

He shook his head. 'You mustn't think that I'm unfeeling. I'm in favour of doing something about it at home. I vote for people who want to do something. But sometimes I wonder if anything can be done. Sometimes

I think this is just impossible. There are too many people. There are swarms and swarms of people wanting a place in the lifeboat.'

'You think that?'

'Yes, I do. There are too many Indians for India to support. It's as simple as that. India's a rich country in many ways. We can launch a satellite. We have great industries. Everything. But it's still such a battle for most people. That's why, if one wants to get anywhere, one tries to get out. Look at all the computer scientists and doctors and people who have gone to the United States. They go and they never come back. They advertise in *The Times of India* for a bride and they start their families over there. And every one of them, every one, thinks: thank God I'm out of India.'

He looked at his wine glass. 'You know something?' he said. 'I don't know whether people here understand how we feel in India. We look at your life – the life you lead in the West, where everything is clean and works and you have money, and we say to ourselves, Me too. I want that too. I want to be there.

'And wouldn't you feel the same? If you were one of those people in Bombay, let's say a teacher, working for maybe eight thousand rupees a month and seeing that somebody in Sydney or London or somewhere like that is getting paid ten, fifteen times as much for the same work, or less work even. What would you want to do?'

She smiled. 'I'd want to get out of Bombay.'

'Yes,' he said. 'You would.'

She thought for a moment. 'The global village . . .'

'Yes,' he said. 'But villages can be very difficult places to live in, can't they?'

6

She had cooked pasta, because that was what she had in the flat that Sunday. They talked as she served it onto his plate and refilled his glass of wine. She told him that she had been engaged, briefly, to an engineer in the oil industry. They had discovered after a few months that they were unsuited to one another and had parted good friends.

'I'm quite happy by myself,' she said. 'I find that I appreciate the freedom. I can come in when I like and go out when I like. At weekends I sometimes don't do anything, just eat out of a tin and read the papers. I don't have to feel guilty about that.'

He said, 'I prefer to be with people, and so it is very difficult for me here. I suppose that I will make friends, but I don't know how to go about it. Where am I going to meet people? If I go to the Indian community, they'll just try to marry me off. That's the first thing they think of. Marriage. And salaries. I mentioned *The Times of India* and its marriage supplement. It has columns just for doctors, you know. Doctors looking for doctors, or people looking for doctors to marry their daughters. That's how people think.'

She said, 'We have our equivalent. We call them lonely hearts columns. They're very funny.'

He looked surprised. 'Why should they be funny?'

She shrugged. 'Oh, I don't know. Don't you think that there's something really rather odd about people advertising themselves, saying that they've got a good sense of humour, saying that they like to go to the cinema, and so on. Funny and a bit tragic, I suppose.'

He did not see what was funny about that. Why should people not describe themselves or what they did? Was it odd to enjoy going to the cinema, and to say as much?

'I can see that you're puzzled,' she said. 'Our sense of what's amusing can be a bit strange, I suppose. You'll get used to it, though. You'll soon be laughing at things which you never would have thought funny before. You'll get the joke.'

7

He saw her again the next day, as he came back from work. He was at the bottom of the stair, and she was coming down. They greeted one another, and he moved aside for her to walk past him. She did so, smiling at him, and then, immediately afterwards, she paused. He had started to climb the stairs, but stopped after he had taken one step.

'That was kind of you to invite me last night,' he said. 'I enjoyed the meal.'

She made a self-deprecatory gesture. 'It wasn't anything special,' she said. 'Pasta was all I had. Next time I'll do something better for you. What would you like?'

'I'd be happy with anything,' he said. 'I'm not fussy.'

'Good.' She hesitated, and then said, 'Well, goodbye.'

He did not want her to go. 'Or I could cook for you,' he said hurriedly. 'This bag here. It's got some rice in it and I can make a sauce. I could . . .'

She smiled encouragingly. 'That would be very nice. When? Tonight?'

'Why not?'

She complimented him on his cooking, although he told her that what he had prepared was very simple. Then, after they had finished the meal, she looked at her watch and suggested that they might just make a film she was keen to see at the Filmhouse, if he was interested, that is. He accepted readily, and they walked round the corner to catch a bus.

They alighted at the end of Princes Street, walking round the corner to Lothian Road. Although it was a Monday, and quite early, there was a small crowd of people, fired up with drink, standing outside a bar, arguing about admission. The bouncers, with their pugilists' physique, stood squarely in the doorway. One of the crowd turned and looked at him as they walked past.

She muttered, 'Don't make eye contact.' But he had already met the man's gaze, and saw the expression on his face. He turned away quickly, and looked across the road to the imposing financial building; glass and stone, rational, reliable. And behind him that sudden glimpse of what seemed to be hatred, or anger perhaps. Why? Did he think he was a Muslim? Was that it? Was that man, with his look of loathing, one of those people who hated Muslims because of everything that had happened? And what if I really was a Muslim and knew that the hate was real and was directed at me for what I was, not a mistaken hate like this?

A few yards further on she said, 'This is a pretty disgusting place at night.'

'Why do people drink so much?' he asked. 'In India
. . .' He did not complete his sentence. It was rude to
criticise; he was a guest.

'They don't drink as much in India? I'm not surprised.
It's our national failing.' She paused. 'We've turned into
a country of foul-mouthed louts. Aggressive. Pickled in
alcohol. Welcome to modern Scotland.'

He was not sure whether he was meant to take this
seriously. He looked at her and she nodded. 'It's true,' she
said. 'It really is.'

The trouble is, he thought, that one never knows
whether what they say is what they mean. A person could
say it's true and mean the direct opposite, and the person
to whom the remark was made would know what was
meant. His uncle, the enthusiast for English, had said,
'English is very clear. That is why it is such a useful
language. It is clear and precise.' That is what he had said;
but that particular uncle had never been out of India. The
sort of British people he had spoken to all his life were
probably those who had lived in India for some time.
Those were people who usually believed in something;
old-fashioned people, who meant what they said.

8

The following Saturday, she offered to take him for a
drive.

'My car is rather old and it doesn't always start,' she
said. 'But it should get us there and back. Just.'

They followed the road south and turned off just before Tranent, heading for the coast of East Lothian. It was a fine late autumn day, one of those days in which the weather seemed to apologise for its behaviour over the summer, when the sun returned, but was more distant, weaker, and made the light seem so clear. He looked out across fields that had been cut back to stubble, over the Forth which was dark blue and slightly choppy. The light foreshortened distance, and made the huddle of hills that was Fife seem barely a mile or two away. A ship, a tanker, rode at anchor, wavelets breaking white against her bow.

He searched for words that would describe what he saw. The word, clean, came to mind, but Kerala too, or parts of it, was clean. Scrubbed, perhaps. No, that was not it. And then he realised that the word he was looking for was northern. He had seen light like this up in Himachal Pradesh, near Shimla, when he had gone with a group of young doctors for a ministry of health conference on infectious diseases. They had stayed in a cheap hotel perched on a mountainside and when he had gone back to his room one afternoon and opened the shutters he had seen light like this. It had brought the distant mountains, briefly revealed, so close that one might feel one might walk to them.

They drove through North Berwick and down a road that ended in a small parking place under a circle of tall trees. There was a path which she seemed to know quite well, and she led him confidently down this towards the sand dunes. Since they had left the car the wind had risen, and he felt it against his brow and in his hair. He had only a thin pullover and he was feeling chilly, in spite of the sun, which was on the wind-bent grass, making it gold.

It was such a different sea, cold, without that smell which the sea had at home. There were birds wheeling and dipping over the waves and crabs that scuttled sideways as they approached them along the tide-line.

His hand brushed against hers, briefly, but she looked up at him when it happened. He pretended not to notice. He had not planned that anything like this should happen, that he should walk, by himself, along a beach in Scotland with a woman who was his neighbour, and that his hand should brush against hers.

She said, 'We can walk along as far as those rocks over there. You see them? Those ones. Then we can go back to the car along another path.'

He smiled. 'I'm getting a bit cold,' he said. 'I should have brought my jacket.'

'Yes,' she said. 'I told you, didn't I? You can't trust this country. Everything changes, just like that. You think it's warm and then suddenly it's cold.'

Over the next few weeks, they slipped into an easy routine. She would come and knock on his door in the early evening and they would decide who would do the cooking. Sometimes they went out, and ate in a restaurant a couple of streets away. They watched films together. She sometimes just called in to talk, to unburden herself of some office row, some misunderstanding. He told her about the people at work, and the things they said. He tried to explain the project, in non-scientific terms, and she tried to understand. But the picture that she had in her mind was of him bending over his microscope, turning the focus button. She could not imagine what it would be like to look at cells all day. But he seemed to her to be a hero, locked in a battle to discover the building blocks of life.

He slowly found out more about her; that she had been born in Penicuik and had gone to school there; that her father was a civil servant who had something to do with agriculture and grants for farmers; that her mother cut people's hair at home; that she had a sister who had gone to live in London and worked for a commercial radio station down there. She told him about her time at Napier University, when she lived in a student flat above a pizza parlour, and that the flat smelled permanently of mozzarella and basil, but that nobody minded this, but got used to it.

One of the people at work, the research fellow who was rudest to the Professor, said to him, as they drank coffee in the small staffroom at the end of the corridor, 'I see you have a girlfriend now. She looks nice.'

He had looked at him in puzzlement, and then realised.

'I saw you at that restaurant,' his colleague went on. 'Somebody you met here?'

He looked down at the floor. He had always felt bashful about these things. Was there something wrong with him? Other people spoke about these matters very openly, but he had never done that. He had been shy.

'She's my neighbour,' he said. 'Her flat is downstairs from mine.'

The colleague nodded. 'Good. Maybe bring her round some time. Helen and I would like to have you round for supper. You can bring your friend.'

He waited for the invitation to become more specific, but it did not, and he concluded that this was one of those invitations that were really not meant to be taken seriously. It was a friendly way of talking; that was all.

When he went home that day, he thought about her. He wondered what it was that existed between them. Nothing had happened, nothing in that sense, but he found that he had no desire for anything like that to happen. She was a friend, a neighbour; she was not a lover. He tried to imagine her as his lover, but could not. She was like a sister, really. It was a platonic relationship, a friendship between a man and a woman of the sort that sometimes blossoms in exactly these circumstances, between neighbours. He remembered how, on that Saturday in East Lothian, his hand had brushed against hers, and that he had seen her looking at him, as if expecting him to do something, which of course he did not. He did not do anything because he felt that it would be like touching a male friend. He did not want to do it; the desire to do so was simply absent.

He thought that it might be different for her. She seemed fond of him; she wanted to spend time in his company. But if she felt attached to him in that way, then he would have somehow to make it clear that this was not the way he felt. That could be difficult. He could hardly say to her explicitly that he was not interested in her; she might laugh at him and ask him whatever gave him the idea that she felt anything like that for him. That was the way many girls would react to that; and under-standably so; they had their pride.

He felt flushed and uncomfortable just to think about

it, and later that evening, when she came to his door to ask him if he wanted to share dinner he toyed with the idea of pretending to be out, but his hall light was on and she would have seen it shining from under the door. That night she asked him whether he would like to go to Glasgow with her the following Sunday. She would drive and they could visit the Burrell Collection. He hesitated. He wanted to decline, but he could not find the words, and he said that he would like that. She seemed pleased.

9

When he had gone down to Cochi to see his family before he came to Scotland, his mother had given him a large album, bound in artificial red leather. It was the sort of album in which wedding photographs were stored and then tucked away in a drawer. On the cover of this album, though, were the words, engraved in gold, My Family. To remind you, she said. However far you travel, there is still your family. Always. No place like home, remember that.

He had opened it in front of everyone and turned over the stiff black boards that were the pages of the album. On each page she had mounted a colour photograph of some member of the family, starting with his grand-parents, his grandmother in a red sari, his grandfather in grey trousers and a plain white kurta. And then his parents at their wedding, a photograph he knew well, standing outside the tiny church with its large wrought-iron gate on which the words The Church of St Thomas, God be with You had been worked. And there was his favourite uncle, the one who so loved the English language, sitting on his verandah, a book, appropriately enough, in his hands; and he could make out what the book was, Palsgrave's *Golden Treasury*.

He was vaguely embarrassed about the album. It seemed so sentimental to have something called My Family, and he could not imagine any of the people at work having such a thing. It was naïve, he supposed; like the work of one of those artists who painted one-dimensional people against a background deprived of perspective. But now he took it out from the cupboard in which he had placed it, wrapped up in a plastic bag, and opened it. Towards the back was a picture of his cousin, Francesca. The photograph had been taken in a photographer's studio, against a background of what appeared to be painted clouds. It was as if Francesca was flying and had been chanced upon by the photographer. Even her hair seemed to be swept back, as if by the wind of her flight.

Francesca was an attractive girl, a couple of years younger than he was. They had been friends throughout their childhood and he was pleased when she became engaged to a boy he had known at school, the very same boy who had given him that theological advice all those years ago.

He looked at Francesca, and smiled. She could do him a service now, and he did not think that she would mind. Carefully he edged the photograph out of its restraining corners. Then he measured it and noted down the measurements. There was a store round the corner which he had noticed sold picture frames. It was run by a woman who sat behind the counter, reading a newspaper. She was always there, and he had never seen her do any business, not once. Tomorrow he would go in and buy a frame.

He looked at the photograph of his cousin and on impulse kissed it. Francesca was different from Jen. He had always wanted to kiss his cousin, right from the time they were small children. But he had never done it, although one evening, while they were sitting together on the verandah playing cards, she suddenly leaned over and kissed the top of his head.

'You smell of coconut oil,' she said.

He was not sure, at eleven, if that was a compliment, but it left him burning. And even now he remembered it with all the delight with which one remembers an illicit pleasure, a moment of intense erotic excitement. That was what he wanted. He wanted somebody like her, like Francesca, who would remind him of those days, and who he really was. It would just have to be somebody like that; not somebody who came from this place, with its lack of colour, and its cold evenings, and its thin light.

The following day, he bought the frame and slipped the picture inside it. The frame was silver, or plated with something that might have been silver, and it gave the photograph of Francesca a certain dignity. She was an attractive woman, his cousin, and he was proud of her, of her fair complexion, as the matrimonial advertisement would have it, and of the filigree necklace she wore about her neck in the photograph, which was delicate and in good taste.

He spent some time finding the right place for the photograph. It should not be too prominently displayed, because that, he thought, would look odd, almost as if he was trying to convey a message. There was a small table in the hall, a table that was used for keys and bits of paper, but that was not the place for it. Nor would it go on the small mantelpiece above the gas fire in the living room; again that was too obvious. So he settled for the kitchen, on the shelf immediately above the sink. She went there to fill the kettle or to help him wash up after they had eaten together. If he pushed it back a bit, it would look natural.

He looked at Francesca. Her gaze met his, and he felt a momentary pang. She would not have done this herself. Why can't you just be honest? she had said to him once, about something or other, and he had been silenced by the question. Was he dishonest? He did not think he was, but if she saw him now she would surely laugh and say, There you are! And now you're making me dishonest too.

Two days later he rang her doorbell and invited her to join him for supper. He felt his heart beating hard within him as he spoke. She smiled at him and accepted. 'I've brought you something about the Burrell,' she said. 'You can look at it before we go over there. Here.'

She handed him a soft-covered book with a picture of an imposing vase on the front. He looked at it, ashamed that he was doing this. Art was all about truth, was it not? And here he was trying to mislead her; to mislead a friend. But he did not want to hurt her; he did not want that. This was the easiest way.

She arrived for the meal. She came into the kitchen

to help him carry the plates through, and he thought for a moment that she had seen the photograph, but she had not. In the sitting room, a small room with only three chairs and a small table, they ate with the plates on their lap. She spoke about something which had happened at work, a row between her supervisor and a new employee that had resulted in an exchange of insults. He found it strange that somebody could speak to an employer like that and get away with it. He remembered the rudeness of the research fellow, who had now taken to sighing audibly when the Professor spoke. People were less respectful here, he thought. No, they were rude. That was all it was, rudeness. And he had expected everything to be so correct, so clean, so well-run. It was clean and well-run, he thought, but it was not correct.

'You're quiet this evening,' she said. 'Is everything all right?'

His reply came quickly. 'Yes. Yes. Everything is all right.'

She looked at him sideways. 'I'm not sure if I always know what you're thinking,' she said. 'You go quiet like that. You frown. You look like this. Like this. See.'

She laughed, and he could not help but smile. He knew that he had a tendency to frown, and that others might find that amusing.

Suddenly she reached out and placed her hand on his, gently. 'You see, I think of you as being . . . as being an exotic, I suppose. Does that sound odd? That's how they describe plants that are from somewhere else. Exotics.'

He stared at her. The pressure of her hand on his was light, but he felt his skin becoming hot. He wanted to move his hand, to take it away from her, but he did not. He did not look down at her hand. He said nothing. He was quiet.

From outside, on the stair, there came the sound of voices. There was a man upstairs who was a bit deaf. He spoke to his wife in a raised voice, like a drill sergeant giving an order. She shouted back at him, her voice rising shrilly with the effort.

'There they go,' she said. 'I suppose they don't know that we can hear every word.'

He smiled weakly and moved his hand away, to pick up the plates. 'I have a dessert for us,' he said. 'It's an Indian dessert. I think you will like it. It has ice cream and a sort of nut sauce. Do you like both of those?'

She rose to her feet. 'I love them,' she said.

They walked through to the kitchen and he put the dirty plates down beside the sink. He moved to one side, to let her get past, and he knew the moment that she saw the photograph.

At first she said nothing. She was holding the kettle, which she was about to fill at the sink. She poised, her hand upon the tap but not turning it. Then slowly she took off the kettle lid and began to fill the kettle with water. She turned round, and saw that he was watching her. He should have looked away, in order to make it less obvious, but he was unable to move. It was as if he had set a trap for a small, defenceless creature, and the creature had fallen in. And now it was too late to do anything about it.

'That's a new photo,' she said, her voice quiet and even.

He was sure that his nervousness showed. 'Oh that,' he said. 'Yes. It was in . . . it was in a cupboard. I had been meaning to put it out.'

She half-turned and looked again at the photograph. 'Who is it?'

He swallowed. 'It's a girl,' he said.

She forced a laugh. 'So I see. But who?'

He looked away; it was easier to lie if one looked away. 'She's called Kitty da Silva. Those names – Portuguese names – are quite common in Cochi. The da Silvas are Indian now, but they have those names from back then.'

She crossed the room to plug in the kettle. 'What does Kitty da Silva do?'

He thought quickly. She was a nurse. No, she was not. She was a teacher, perhaps. It would be better for her to be a teacher. A nurse would be too obvious. 'She teaches at a school,' he said. 'It's a small school for . . . for small children. That is what she does.'

'Have you known her long?' she asked, and then added, almost as an afterthought, 'I assume that she's special to you. Having her photograph. I didn't know . . .'

He still could not look at her. 'I must tell you more about her one day.' And then, with forced cheerfulness, 'That dessert I told you about. It's in the fridge. Let me get the plates. No, don't you bother. I'll get them.'

10

He did not see her the next day, nor the day after that. He went down to knock on her door, hesitantly and full of guilt, but there was no reply. He thought that he heard a sound within, but could not be sure. He

ALEXANDER McCALL SMITH

wondered about looking through the letter-box, but realised that if she were in and saw him he would just compound their mutual awkwardness. And so he went up to his flat and sat there, unable to concentrate on the work that he had brought home with him, some scientific papers that he had to read. They had a team meeting in a couple of days and they were going to talk about the recent literature. But he could not absorb what he was reading, and sometimes he would get to the end of an article and realise that he had taken nothing in.

He had distanced himself from her, he reflected, and he had done it without anything being said. There had been no awkward exchange of regrets; nothing had been said. And, most importantly, she should not feel rejected by him. He did not want that.

But he missed her, and in the days that followed he found that he thought of her at odd moments. He knocked again on the door of her flat, but this time he was sure that she was not there, and he went upstairs wondering what she was doing. He assumed that the projected trip to Glasgow and the Burrell was off. And who could blame her if she did not want to do that.

Then, the next day, when he went home, he found a note through his door. I have to go to Dundee for a couple of days, the note read. But I shall be back on Saturday, quite late. Is Sunday still all right for Glasgow? Let me know if it isn't. Leave a message at the office. They know where I am.

He finished reading the note and felt a sudden surge of joy. It was the feeling that he used to get when he saw his name on the pass list at medical school; a curious, light-hearted exhilaration. He went to the window and looked out onto the street. There were a few people about, and he felt a sudden, inexplicable affection for them, these people he did not know. One looked up and saw him. He wanted to wave, to call out, but they did not do that in this city. They must have their moments of joy, he supposed, but there were no processions here, no dancing in the streets, no flinging of coloured powder.

They walked about the Burrell. She had been quiet – not cold, but quiet. In the car on the way across she had talked about Dundee and about work. There had been no silences, but she was still quieter than usual. He found himself happy just to be in her company. He wanted to say sorry, to explain, but he could not. He would think of something in due course. He could talk and tell her. One could always be honest.

They sat and had coffee together.

'How could one man collect all this?' she said. 'Isn't it extraordinary?'

'He must have been very rich.'

'He was. Ships. People with ships can be very wealthy. Those Greeks.'

'There are ship-owners in Cochi too. Big men. Very big.'

She traced a pattern with her spoon in the milky foam of her coffee. He strained to see what the design was. A flower, perhaps, or just a twirling like those Celtic inter-twinings he had seen and which seemed to him to be so beautiful, like the border of a Mughal manuscript. Artists

ALEXANDER McCALL SMITH

are brothers, he thought; across the years, the centuries. Brothers.

'How is Kitty da Silva?' she asked suddenly. 'How is she?'

He said nothing for a moment; a silence of the human heart.

'She is no more,' he said.

She looked up with a start. 'No more?'

'She went for a walk in the forest up in the hills,' he said. 'She was eaten by a tiger.'

She looked at him in astonishment, and then, under-standing, she began to laugh.

Showtime

IAN RANKIN

There's a crowd of about a thousand watching him. Biggest audience he's ever had, and ever likely to have. And here he is, rooted to the spot. Old Mesmer the Magician couldn't have done a better job. Thing about hypnosis, sometimes it was real, sometimes they'd use a ringer. Because there was a difference between magic and illusion. That was the point most of the best-known ones made these days. Guys like Penn and Teller, they even showed you how the trick was done. Well, sometimes they did. Then you got the double-bluff where they'd explain to you what you thought was the trick, only to have some other trick backing it up – bigger than the first and even more impossible.

And just as a hypnotist needed someone who was willing to be put under, so every illusionist needed a 'mark' – that was what the pros called them – someone pulled from the crowd to help with the trick. Thing was, the mark had to be gullible. They fell under the spell of the trick and helped it work. Sometimes by masking what the magician was really up to, or taking attention away. He'd seen it last summer on the High Street. Fringe time, a sunny day. He'd sold the last of his *Big Issue*s and was just passing time. Plenty of free shows up and down the High Street: jugglers and singers and mimes. Actors handing out flyers. He'd watched an acrobat on a twelve-foot tall unicycle. Tossing sticks into the air and catching them. Started dropping them. People clapped in sympathy.

'Don't clap till I get it right!' he'd yelled. Then asked a blonde at the front of the crowd to throw them back up to him. Eventually explained that the only reason he kept dropping the sticks was so he had an excuse to look down the front of her T-shirt. That got the crowd laughing, but what Tiger couldn't work out was whether this was the usual routine, or the acrobat had been covering up for his mistakes.

Still thinking about it as he sauntered past packed cafés. The pavement tables were busy, and he'd considered asking for spare change, but knew he shouldn't: *Big Issue* seller, working not begging. All the same, selling the mag was getting tougher. He had a couple of pitches, strict time limits on both. Some guys just stood there, looking sorry for themselves. Others tried too hard, scared the punters off. Tiger had his regulars, the ones who'd stop for a blether, maybe hand over more than the quid cover price. Sometimes they gave him a coffee from the nearby stall. The woman on the stall had what his mum would have called a heart of gold – bacon roll every morning, nothing to pay. Walking past those cafés, he felt peckish. Cash in his pocket, but the prices here would be too steep. Stopped instead at the edge of another crowd by St Giles. He'd only paused to hawk into the middle of the Heart of Midlothian – supposed to be lucky, but what he really liked was the look of disgust on the faces of the tourists. But then the man's voice caught him, drew him in, and he found himself watching a master at work.

Life-changing, he'd later describe it. Absolutely life-changing.

The man's name was Domino. Not Fats Domino, as he told the crowd, patting his stomach. John Domino. Not his real name – that way he could body-swerve the taxman. This appealed to Tiger – who hadn't been born Tiger, after all. Tigger, that's what they'd called him at school, the few years he'd actually gone to school. He kept bouncing all over the place, so they gave him the name. 'Go on, Tigger, bounce for us,' and that's exactly what he'd do. It was like there was electricity inside him instead of blood. High spirits, his mum said. But the schools and the authorities didn't agree. Way they looked at him, he was different enough to be difficult. Needed tablets to earth all that excess energy, the way the doctors described it. But the name had stuck by then, changed to Tiger as he got older.

All of which he would eventually tell John Domino. But first they had to meet. And Tiger was keen to meet Domino once he'd watched him in action, watched him pick a mark from the crowd and work around him – young tourist called Andy from Australia. Domino standing close by Andy's shoulder, asking him questions, working around him, shaking hands, patting his arms and commenting on his muscular physique, working around him, asking him where he bought his jacket, looked waterproof, what was it he'd heard about the Scottish weather? Talking and moving, his mouth as fast as his hands. The mark grinning, knowing something was going on. Something was going on all right. Domino reached a hand from behind Andy's head to show the crowd he'd taken the tourist's watch. Next came a passport and wallet. He asked Andy the time, gave him back his watch and told him to strap it on. Thirty seconds later Domino was holding it up again, and had swiped a thick leather belt from the mark's waistband. Bang–bang–bang . . . it was so fast and yet so controlled. It was . . . the only word for it was mesmerising.

Big round of applause for Andy, then a few card tricks and a chickpea hidden under one of three cups. Five quid offered to anyone who worked out where the chickpea was. Eventually someone got it right and Domino handed them the fiver. Round of applause and, as they turned away, Domino showed the crowd that the note was back in his own hand. He took a collection, not everybody chipping in. Most moving away as soon as he started asking. But Tiger stood there, and eventually Domino was in front of him. The man looked at him and seemed to know. Gave a wink and said not to worry.

'I want to . . .' Tiger began saying, bringing out a hard-earned pound coin.

'I know you do, son,' the magician told him, 'and that's more than enough for me.'

Afterwards, Tiger had started in at him with the questions, the pair of them walking. How did he learn to do it? What else could he do? And then the biggie, as far as Tiger was concerned – with all that skill, why wasn't he down Waverley Station picking pockets? Domino had turned to him, smile dropping from his face.

'I'm not a crook, son, and I'd rather not see the inside of a jail cell. How about you?'

'Banged up once or twice,' Tiger admitted.

'Fun, was it?'

'The tea was better than you get at the shelter.'

'So what do you do now?'

'I sell the *Big Issue*. Thing is, if I could do what you do . . . even a fraction of it . . .'

'It's not the easiest profession to break into, son.'

'Just a few tricks, that's what I mean . . . help me sell the mag. You know, provide a bit of a show.'

Domino had thought for a moment. 'I could show you the basics. But then you'd have to practise.'

'No problem.'

They were at South Bridge by now, Domino looking up and down the street.

'Magic Circle says I'm not supposed to.'

'Who am I going to tell?'

Domino was pointing with a long, thin finger. 'Festival Theatre's just along there, right?'

'That's right.'

'Then that's your part of the bargain.'

'What is?'

'The Great Lafayette. We'll go see him. Then maybe you'll understand . . .'

A thousand spectators . . . blue skies . . . shouts of encouragement. And he's in this sort of trance. Call it stage fright, except it isn't. It's more like he's not really there. Princes Street Gardens in July. The G8's been and gone; the Festival's just around the corner. Been a mad enough summer already and here he is in the middle of it. There's an artificial pitch under his feet, and over a dozen different languages ringing in his ears. Castle Rock as a backdrop, faces hanging over the ramparts.

'Tiger, ya dozy get!'

'Whass up wi' him?'

'Wakey-wakey, Tiger. Did you miss your Frosties or something?'

Eight of them . . . four men either team. One side from Scotland, the other Russian. The Homeless World Cup, first round, and they all know his bottle's gone. That he can't hack it.

'Been at the jellies, Tiger?' someone's shouting.

'This is a football pitch, no' a *Big Issue* pitch, ya choob. You're supposed to move about a bit!'

This last called out by the Scotland coach. The forty-a-day voice breaks the spell, just as a Russian's making to pass Tiger with the ball. He sticks out a sluggish leg and trips the guy. Referee's on his whistle, coach stretching his arms skywards as if asking the Big Man what he's done to deserve this. The Russian – skinny, gaunt-cheeked, cropped black hair (bit like Zidane actually) is staring up at Tiger, scowling. Funny thing is, there's a drawing of a tiger on his shirt, its mouth open in a roar. The Russian team are called S P Tigers – the S P stands for St Petersburg.

'Sorry, pal,' Tiger offers, reaching out a hand. The player takes it and gets to his feet. Tiger pats him on the shoulder. But now the Russian is being eased aside by the ref, who has eyes only for Tiger: eyes, a red card, and a single word.

'Off!'

Which has the squad and most of the partisan crowd howling their disagreement. But Tiger makes no fuss; just jogs to the nearest hoarding and clambers over. The coach is yelling that the goalie's going to have to play

IAN RANKIN

defence, too, leaving just the one midfielder and one forward.

'Sorry, boss,' Tiger says, but he's cold-shouldered. Anger wells in him and he glares at the man. Nice watch on his wrist: Tiger could probably have it off him. Cash in his tracksuit pockets: he could have that as well. But then he remembers that first meeting with Domino, and the words of warning, and the moment passes. 'Really sorry,' he says, to no one in particular. Then he stands beside the subs, and pretends to watch the game.

'The Great Lafayette,' Domino was saying. They'd pushed open the doors of the Festival Theatre. No one had looked at them or challenged them as they'd started climbing the staircase. Couple of staff manning the box office; tables in the café busy. But as they climbed, they passed no one. Tiger was breathing heavily as they reached the third landing. Domino pointed to a wall, and led him towards it. Framed pictures, pages taken from a theatre programme. Here was Tiger's side of the bargain: he was to learn about the Great Lafayette.

Took him a while; reading never his strong point. Some of the words made no sense, but the gist did. Lafayette had been one of the best magicians of his day. He was known as the 'man of mystery', and toured the world with a forty-strong company, plus lions and horses. The show arrived in Edinburgh in 1911, and was due to play two weeks at the Empire Palace Theatre, Nicolson Street. Lafayette did things with style – stayed at the Caledonian, as did his dog Beauty. Beauty had its own room, own bed. Tiger had to laugh at that. Wasn't so happy when he got to the bit about the lion though. It would appear onstage in its cage and start roaring, but only because the floor of the cage was electrified.

'Cruelty to animals,' Tiger muttered.

'That was the age he lived in,' Domino reasoned. 'You'll see one of his acts was called "The Evolution of the Negro". It was an illusion where a black man becomes white.'

'What's the "Electric Sousa"?'

'A robot supposedly. An actor in disguise, to be precise.' Domino taps the glass. 'Despite the cruelty, he did love his dog . . .'

But Beauty had died soon after the show's arrival in Edinburgh – taken to be a bad omen by its owner. And then, on the night of 9 May, with Lafayette waiting in the wings, disguised as a lion, the set had caught fire. Audience got out, but the cast and crew weren't so lucky. Ten deaths, among them the illusionist himself. Cremated in Glasgow and the ashes brought back to Edinburgh. But meantime, in the basement of the theatre, the real Lafayette's remains had turned up. His stunt double from the lion illusion had been cremated in his place.

'He was buried in Piershill,' Tiger said aloud.

'Alongside Beauty,' Domino added. 'Houdini sent a wreath.'

Tiger just nodded: a wreath, yes, shaped like a dog's head. Because Beauty had been a gift to Lafayette from Houdini himself. Tiger straightened up.

'I never knew any of this,' he said.

'You know it now.'

'And that's my side of the bargain?'

'I suppose it is, which means I need to keep mine. So . . . what is it you want to know?'

Answer? Everything. But Domino had shaken his head. Started Tiger off that day with a bit of juggling, using three apples bought at the café. They went to the Meadows to practise, found a patch of grass behind the circus tent. Some juggling, then a few basic card tricks and the cups-and-chickpea routine. The few breaks they'd taken, Domino had told stories about the great illusionists, given a few tips on how to work a crowd.

'I do hotels sometimes,' he'd explained. 'Sunday lunches, families tucking into the all-you-can-eat buffet. I'm paid to work the tables, lifting keys from pockets, making stuff appear and disappear. You want to see close magic, you could do worse than buy a ticket for Jerry Sadowitz – he's playing the Fringe somewhere. If you want to take things further, there's a shop in Glasgow, sells props. The pros use it like a supermarket.'

The sun dying gently behind them as they talked and worked. A handshake at day's end, Domino turning down Tiger's offer of a pint.

'So what's on the cards for tomorrow?' Tiger had asked, still keen, head buzzing.

'What indeed?' Domino had replied.

'Will I see you up the High Street, or do you want to meet here?'

Domino had just shrugged and smiled, and Tiger had known he wouldn't be seeing him the next day, or any other day. Couldn't explain how he knew this; he just did.

'Psychology, that's what it boils down to,' Domino had said a couple of hours before. 'Basic understanding of people. Best learned by watching them.'

'That's what I do all day,' Tiger had replied, as Domino had nodded slowly. And as his teacher started to leave, Tiger felt a pang of hunger for the first time since the High Street. Picked up one of the apples and bit into it, then tossed it into the air, eyes fixed ahead of him. Caught it and tossed it again, this time adding a second. The third he wasn't so sure about: it was covered in dirt from being dropped so often.

Full-time and somehow the Scots have scraped a draw. Tiger gets dirty looks from his three team-mates. He's holding a football in the palm of one hand, wondering how the hell he can juggle three of them. Reckons it could be done . . . with enough practice.

Practice hadn't come easy to him, even after Domino's masterclass. He'd stumbled a few times, given it up as a joke. But then he'd think of Lafayette, and Lafayette's custom Mercedes with its little statue of Beauty above the grille. Man of mystery all right: in real life he was a German Jew called Neuberger. Some people said he'd gone back onto the stage to rescue his horse. Tiger had been to the library on George IV Bridge, done a search on Lafayette. The librarian helpful, not seeming to mind that Tiger didn't look like a student or professor. Lafayette's show had included midgets dressed as robots and teddy bears – two of them had died in the Edinburgh fire. Another act had involved catching pigeons in mid-flight. Tiger guessed they'd probably been attached to lengths of thread. You used the same thing in some card tricks: the right card levitating from the pack. You could place a coin on the face of a card then make the coin float in the air – tiny threads supporting it as you flexed the card.

No money for props, so he started making some of his own. Had to buy a pack of cards – in fact, had to buy three identical packs. Some tricks demanded doublers. Got good at shuffling. One of the regulars at the night shelter on Holyrood Road, turned out he was a croupier in his twenties. Hands shaky now, but still able to show Tiger how to do a nifty shuffle. Fingers becoming dexterous, confidence growing. At first, he fluffed as many tricks as he got right. His punters didn't seem to mind too much. Might smile in sympathy or out of embarrassment.

'Don't smile till I get it right,' he'd tell them. Then he'd pull a coin from behind their kid's ear, or make a stick of chewing gum disappear from his clenched hand. When things were slow, he might juggle. He had three tennis balls – found them down by the courts on the Meadows, stuck high up in the fencing or else tucked deep in the surrounding hedges. Hadn't graduated to clubs, didn't know where he could get any.

'That's the last game you get,' someone is snarling at him. It's the forward, rubbing sweat from his hair with a towel. He looks to the coach. 'That better be right, boss, or I'm walking, swear to God and Dennis Law.'

'We'll see,' is all the coach says. 'But well done, lads, anyway: fighting spirit, that's what's got us here.'

He falls quiet as one of the Russian players approaches.

It's the one who looks a bit like Zidane. He's holding out his hand for Tiger to shake. Tiger takes it and nods. The coach starts clapping.

'Well done, son. Bit of sportsmanship never goes amiss.' He slaps the Russian on the back.

'Arkady,' the player says, eyes still on Tiger.

'Tiger,' comes the reply. Their hands are still clasped.

'Get a room, the pair of you,' the forward mutters from beneath his towel.

'Pollock Halls?' the Russian asks. Tiger understands. It's where the teams are staying. He nods to let the man know he'll see him there; mimes the tipping of a glass to his mouth.

'Many, many,' Arkady says with a grin.

'Many,' Tiger agrees.

'Might as well,' the forward states. 'It's not like you'll be needed back here again . . .'

The refectory building has games machines, and that's where Tiger finds Arkady. He's got the gear-stick in one hand, jabbing at buttons with the other. It's a football tournament, crowd noises coming from the speakers. Tiger reckons Arkady's team are in red. The machine itself is in charge of his black-clad opponents. He soon realises he's wrong.

'Thought you'd be in red,' Tiger says. Arkady doesn't take his eyes off the screen.

'Why?'

'It's the Russian colour, isn't it?'

'Communist colour,' Arkady corrects him. 'You have old idea of Russia.'

Two of Arkady's team-mates saunter past, still in their strips. They call out something to him. When Tiger looks at them, they make waving signs with their fingers, as though holding up red cards. Tiger forces a smile.

'You the only one on your team speaks English?' he asks Arkady.

'Yes.'

'Where did you learn it?'

The Russian pauses as a goal-kick is being taken onscreen. He wipes his palms on his loose jeans. 'Are you a spy?'

Tiger laughs. 'Christ, no, I was only asking . . .'

'Are you a Christian?'

'I'm not really anything.'

'But you use the Christ's name.'

'Only when I'm swearing.'

Arkady goes back to his game and Tiger tries to think of something else to say.

'Funny though, isn't it?' he eventually begins. 'Your team being the Tigers, me being called Tiger.'

The Russian is concentrating on the screen.

'I mean,' Tiger ploughs on, 'it's a big coincidence. Either that or it's meant to happen.' He pauses. 'I've been thinking a lot about that recently, about how coincidences might be signals or something.'

'Signals?' Finally he has the Russian's attention.

'Things that are meant to be,' he clarifies. 'Fate and all that. See, I met this guy a while back . . . well, pretty much exactly a year ago . . . and he was . . . it was like we were meant to meet up, see what I'm saying?'

Arkady is still staring at the screen, but Tiger sees his

reflection there. One man's eyes catching the other's.

'I'm not gay or anything,' Tiger protests, 'if that's what you're thinking.' He watches Arkady shrug. 'It's just that he helped me. Didn't need to, but he did. And I'm still not sure why I even pestered him in the first place. It was me that went to him. I'd no interest in magic before that.'

'Magic?'

'Illusions . . . card tricks . . . all that stuff.' Tiger is looking at the score on the screen. Arkady is playing at the advanced level, and he's 4–0 up. 'You're good at this,' he says.

'I practise.'

'In St Petersburg?'

Arkady nods. 'The shelter has a PlayStation.'

'Aye, some of the shelters here are the same.' Tiger watches the action for a moment.

'You want to play?' the Russian asks.

'Naw, I'm fine. You seem to be doing okay on your own.'

'I meant we could play one another.'

Tiger screws up his face. 'Not really my thing. Just not sure I'm competitive.'

'But you play football?'

'In real life, yeah . . . Tuesday nights . . . five-a-side at Porty if I can scrape the bus fare.'

'Money is a problem.' This is a statement; all Tiger has to do is nod.

'Your English is almost better than mine,' he says instead. 'Were you clever at school?'

'Not really.'

'So where did you learn?'

'In the Army.'

'Thought of joining up myself, once upon a time. Reckoned I might learn a trade, then get invalided out.' Tiger has reached into a pocket for his rolling-tin. He's prised the lid off before he remembers they're not supposed to smoke. Takes a rolly out anyway, offers the tin to Arkady.

'I don't smoke.'

'Must be the only squaddie that doesn't.' Tiger slips the thin, crumpled cigarette between his lips. 'How long were you in for?'

'Six years.'

'See any action?'

'Afghanistan.'

'You winding me up?'

'Winding?'

'Taking the piss . . . having me on . . .'

'I'm not a liar,' the Russian states.

'Bloody hell, Arkady my friend.' Tiger thinks for a moment. 'Don't suppose you brought any Afghan black back with you?'

Cheap day return to Glasgow. Special winter fares. Freezing January, Tiger stumbled into Glasgow. First thing he saw as he left the bus station was a guy punting the *Big Issue*. No sign of a vendor card – they were supposed to keep them prominent. Could mean the guy had found a buckshee bundle of mags; or was holding the fort for a pal. Tiger turned his face away. He was a tourist for today; didn't want anyone recognising a kindred spirit.

Back in August, Domino had mentioned a magic shop in Glasgow. And now that he'd learned some of the tricks of the trade, so to speak, Tiger reckoned he owed it a visit.

The shop itself was anything but imposing. Sat on a quiet side road, off Argyle Street. Window that needed washing; door with a grille on the inside. Place would have looked shut if not for the strip-lighting on the ceiling. Tiger pushed open the door. The interior was narrow. There was a long counter with a glass top, beneath which sat various practical jokes. The shelves behind displayed rubber masks of politicians and movie monsters. Lining the opposite wall was another glass-fronted display-case, this one holding more expensive items. Two men were studying the contents of this case, and Tiger pretended to do the same. He saw a fez and a magic wand, a top hat and 'the knotted handkerchief', and alongside them the equipment needed for card tricks and coin tricks and levitation tricks. There was a woman assistant behind the counter, and she cleared her throat.

'Anything in particular?'

Tiger half-turned towards her. 'Just looking,' he said, surprised by the tremble in his voice. The men were glancing in his direction. One of them carried a pack of cards, and shuffled it elaborately and incessantly.

'Is it fancy dress?' the assistant asked. Tiger shook his head. He'd turned to face the counter. Hot pepper chewing gum; nail-through-the-finger; black soap; fart powder; vampire teeth; whoopee cushion; exploding cigarettes; false eyes; dog poo. 'Do you want a peanut?' She started to prise the lid off a tin. Tiger was reaching out a hand when a green snake shot towards him out of the tin. 'Very popular item,' she explained. Tiger lifted the snake from the floor and handed it back.

'Spring-loaded,' he stated.

'Great fun at parties.'

'Here, son, pick a card,' the man with the deck was saying. He fanned the cards out and Tiger took one. 'Don't show me it, just put it back,' the man instructed.

'What's the point?' Tiger said, holding up the Queen of Hearts. 'They're all the same.'

The man's companion laughed and patted Tiger on the shoulder. 'He's got you there, Alfie,' he said.

Tiger looked at him. 'I've got you, too. Only there was nothing in my jacket pocket for you to lift, was there?'

Now the man with the cards laughed. 'Boy's one of us, Kenny. Not seen you in here before though.'

'I live in Edinburgh.'

'So how did you find us?' the assistant asked.

'Guy called Domino told me.'

'John Domino?' Alfie frowned, slipping the pack of cards into his pocket.

'When was this?'

'You know him?' Tiger asked.

'Used to see him around,' Alfie conceded.

'Years back though,' Kenny added. 'He worked the miners' clubs, up and down the country. Seventies, early eighties. Thought he'd long since snuffed it.'

'I saw him just a few months back.'

'Is he in a home?'

Tiger shook his head. 'He was working the Fringe.'

Kenny's frown deepened. 'At his age?'

'Maybe it's not the same guy,' Tiger said. He went on to describe Domino.

'Sounds like him,' the assistant confirmed.

'His son maybe,' Alfie guessed. 'Old John would have to be in his seventies. No way he'd pass for forty.'

'Unless he's bathing in virgin's blood or something,' Kenny added.

'Might have passed his secrets to a double,' the assistant offered.

Tiger nodded slowly. 'Like Lafayette . . . he used a double for some of his tricks.'

Kenny stared at him. 'Domino was obsessed with Lafayette,' he said quietly. 'When did you say you saw him?'

'This past August.'

Kenny and Alfie shared a look. Tiger realised the assistant had vanished: not in a puff of smoke though. There was a door leading to the shop's back room. It opened and she emerged, carrying a framed picture from which she was blowing dust. 'Look familiar?' she said.

It was the poster for a variety show, dated 1968. Black-and-white photos of the participants: a comedian in bow tie and fancy shirt; ventriloquist with a stuffed bear on his arm; some dancing girls in short skirts . . . and The Mesmeric Domino. The photo was of John Domino, but with a thick moustache and oval-shaped glasses, same kind Lafayette had worn when offstage.

'Spitting image,' Tiger conceded.

'Looks like he's still around then,' the assistant said.

'Did you know him too, then?' Tiger felt bold enough

to ask. She seemed to sense the real question lurking beneath the one he'd voiced. Her eyes were creased with years and too much make-up. Tiger suddenly knew that she'd been a magician's assistant . . . maybe even Domino's assistant. She turned her attention to the poster, said nothing as she went to replace it on its wall.

'Did he take you to see Lafayette?' Kenny asked into the silence. Tiger just nodded. 'You should go back, take another look.' Kenny's hand darted to Tiger's ear, came away again holding a business card, curled at the edges. 'In case you need to get in touch,' he said. Tiger made as if to pocket the card, then flashed his own hand at the man's ear, bringing it out again.

'Boy's good,' Alfie said.

'I had a good teacher.'

'He taught plenty before you,' Kenny stated. The two men locked eyes. Kenny had to be fifty . . . no way John Domino could have had him as a pupil. This time, Tiger pocketed the card. The assistant had returned; looked like she'd been dabbing at her eyes.

'Is there anything special?' she asked, suddenly business-like.

But Tiger knew he could afford none of it. The stage props – the good stuff – had prices into the hundreds of pounds. Even a simple brass cylinder for making coins appear and disappear cost twenty notes. He'd made his pilgrimage, but knew now that he'd have to make his own props, too, using whatever came to hand. He held his palms up in a show of surrender.

'Just looking,' he informed the assistant.

'Have something on us,' Alfie announced, waving a

hand across the display case. 'Any friend of Domino's and all that.' He nudged his friend in the ribs.

'Oh aye,' Kenny spluttered. 'In memory of the great man, who may or may not still be with us.' He seemed to see the price-tags for the first time. 'But go gentle on us, son. It's a tough world out there.'

'You're telling me,' Tiger agreed. Then he pointed to the wand.

Which became his wand. About a foot long, black as ebony with an inch of white tip either end. It came with instructions, and could be extended to twice its length, or shortened to half. It also had a fine filament inside which could be curled round the finger or stuck to the underside of the hand, allowing the wand to levitate or swoop around a stage. He practised with it on the bus home, then couldn't find it next morning. Accused the guy who'd been sleeping in the bed next to him at the shelter. Swung at him and was barred for a week. Wrapped his coat around him and started walking. Should have gone to the *Big Issue* office to pick up a stack of the latest issue, but instead he found himself outside the Festival Theatre. It wasn't open, so he sat on the bench opposite, next to Surgeons' Hall, until it did. Pushed through its doors and climbed the stairs, finding the wall he was looking for. Dragged over a chair and sat down. He read the whole story again, making sense of it as best he could. He still felt sorry for the lion, caged like that and given electric shocks. He imagined it incinerated in the fire. Lafayette had gone back to the stage to rescue his horse. Lafayette had kept his pet dog in a hotel room, pampering it. He was eventually buried with it. Yet no one had mourned the lion. Tiger conjured up images of the lion breaking free, roaming the theatre as flames licked the walls. Sneaking out the back exit and heading for Holyrood Park. Finding refuge there. No more cages or torture. It struck him that the various shelters he used were like zoos, where snorting, restless animals waited till they were sent out into the daylight to perform and beg and be stared at . . .

Then he studied the grainy photograph of Lafayette's company, remembering Kenny's words – take another look. He examined each face. Midgets and musicians and pretty assistants. One of the women actually looked a bit like the woman in the magic shop. And one of the men looked like a younger Alfie. And another could have been related to Kenny . . .

And suddenly Domino was staring back at him. He was next to Lafayette, or, rather, was just behind the great magician's shoulder: similar height and hairstyle. But the text told him this was Charles Richards, Lafayette's double, the man who'd been mourned and cremated in his place. Tiger blinked a few times, let his eyes swim back into focus. Charles Richards, that's who it was.

At a phone-box up by the taxi rank he called the number on Kenny's card. It was answered by a woman, who yelled for Kenny to take the call.

'Hello?' the voice said.

'It's Tiger. We met yesterday.'

'Tiger?' There was a chuckle down the line. 'As good a stage name as any.' Tiger realised no one had asked his name the previous day.

'How's the magic wand?' Kenny was asking. Tiger ignored him.

'I did what you said, took another look at the Lafayette stuff. His double looks just like Domino.'

'Is that right?'

'And there's someone looks like Alfie, too . . . and the shop assistant.'

'Mysteries of the gene pool, young Tiger.'

'What do you mean?'

'Don't go reading too much into it. We're all illusion-ists, aren't we? Doesn't mean we can't sometimes be the mark, too.' The pips sounded; Tiger had no more change.

'You knew I'd see him, didn't you?' he yelled into the receiver. 'He taught you, same as he started teaching me!' Nothing at his ear but the dialling tone. Whether his time was up, or Kenny had put down the phone, he couldn't say.

And the wand never did turn up.

Scotland are playing again, against Austria this time and it's tough going. Fast and furious, and with a guy from Inverness replacing Tiger. He stands with the rest of the squad for a while, then drifts away, ostensibly to light a roll-up. Another nice dry day in Princes Street Gardens. People are lying on the grassy slope with their eyes closed, or sitting along the line of benches, enjoying a blether. And there's Arkady, sitting under a tree, close to the fence behind which runs the railway. There's a bridge somewhere nearby where kids stand while the trains rumble beneath them. Tiger walks over and crouches down.

IAN RANKIN

'Not playing today?'

'This afternoon,' the Russian corrects him. 'What about you?'

Tiger wrinkles his nose. 'Why aren't you with the team?'

'I like to hear the trains.'

'Don't you have trains in Russia?'

'Of course.'

'Tell me about St Petersburg.'

'What's to tell? Sometimes it's cold, sometimes hot.'

'Any jobs to speak of?'

'Not as many as in the past. Under communism, we had full employment – that was the story anyway.'

'You didn't pick up any useful skills in the Army?'

'I learned how to kill.'

'Well, that's a start.' Both men share a laugh.

'The trouble began when I went home after Afghanistan. My papers were supposed to travel separately. They got lost, and without a *propiska* – like a passport – I had no identity. Which means no . . .' He seeks the proper word. 'Entitlements.' He looks to Tiger, who nods to let him know he's doing fine. 'My wife had left me; my family did not want me. I went to the night shelter . . .' He shrugs. 'They have a newspaper called *Put Domoi* . . . it means something like "journey towards home".'

'Like the *Big Issue* here?'

It is Arkady's turn to nod. 'The *nochlezhka* – the night shelter – they now have access to *propiskas*.'

'So you'll finally have your identity back?'

'If I want it.' Arkady stares towards the fence. Tiger can hear the train passing invisibly in the gully behind it. 'Some nights in the shelter, the water freezes. There is no money for bread.' He offers a shrug, then a smile. 'I'm sorry . . .'

'For what?'

'Telling you this, as if it is any worse than your own life.' He gestures in the direction of the pitch. 'Or anybody's life. We are all made of the same stuff, but sometimes cannot see past our own noses.'

Tiger stares at the Russian for what seems to both men a long time. Arkady eventually looks down towards the grass.

'Why don't you want your *propiska*?' Tiger asks quietly. 'Did something happen in Afghanistan?'

'Many things happened in Afghanistan.'

'Is that why your wife left you? Why you couldn't get on with your family?'

Arkady raises his eyes and meets Tiger's stare. 'You are good at reading people's heads, my friend.'

'Some of us are magicians,' Tiger tells him, as if in confidence, 'and when you're a magician, you can make anything happen.' He blows across the palm of his hand. 'Just like that.'

And with a snapping of his fingers, a small red ball appears on the still-outstretched palm. He places his other hand over it for a moment, and the ball is gone. He turns both hands over to let the Russian know he's not hiding it.

'You are clever man, Tiger,' Arkady says.

'Clever enough for some things,' Tiger agrees, as a goal on the pitch is greeted by the home crowd with whistles and cheers.

★

It's their last night at Pollock Halls. Tiger has been working flat-out the past few days, getting everything ready. On breaks from his task, he has walked the corridors, wondering about other routes his life could have taken. Say his dad hadn't hoofed it. Say he'd stuck in at school, kept taking the meds, maybe gone to college or uni. The students who called Pollock Halls home had their own bedrooms. They had a bar and canteen. They had Holyrood Park slap-bang on their doorstep . . .

And what did Tiger have?

Well, he had his wits for one thing. Amazing the stuff you could find in skips. Stuff he lifted, he looked on it as recycling. Bits of wood, nails he could straighten and re-use, even a few half-pots of paint. Old doors and windows provided him with hinges. A nearby DIY store charged only a tenner for their cheapest saw, screwdriver and glue-gun. When one of the campus handymen found out what he was up to, he loaned him a paintbrush, hammer and chisel. The coach had even stuck his head around the door, talking to him again by now.

'Hear you're coming up with something special, Tiger.'

'Hope so.'

'Knew you did card tricks, but.' Tiger just nodding. 'Well, it's looking good, whatever it is.'

High spirits on the day itself. Italy had won for the second year running, beating Poland 3–2 in the final, Scotland finishing a respectable fourth, just behind Ukraine. Even better news for Tiger: wandering unchallenged into one of the older buildings on campus, he'd stood for a moment in its wood-panelled hall, then had opened a door and found himself in some sort of meeting room for the bigwigs. Shields lining the tartan-papered walls.

Shields, with pairs of swords crossed behind them.

Lots of swords.

So now it's the last night and the stage has been set in the recreation hall. He's managed to tweak the stage while no one was around. Takes two other players to help him carry the large box to its position behind the rear curtain.

'Going to saw a lady in half?' one of them asks.

'I don't mind which half I get,' the other laughs.

Big banner above the stage: WORLD CUP PARTY NIGHT 2005. Quite a few have put their names down to do a turn – mostly musical, or telling a joke. One guy reckons he can get the crowd going with his whistled rendition of the theme from *The Good, the Bad, and the Ugly*. The man has no teeth at all in his head, and Tiger isn't sure if this will prove help or hindrance. There'll be women in the audience: friends of the players. Plus all the various coaching staffs and others who've been working behind the scenes. No alcohol, but plenty of soft drinks and stuff to eat. Plus dancing after the show, just to round things off.

Tiger has a ticket in his pocket. Bought it earlier at the Fringe box office: Jerry Sadowitz, close-up magic. A wee treat for himself when August comes. But meantime there's some magic of his own to organise.

Show time . . .

Over two hundred of them in the hall. Lots of clapping and back-slapping. A big meal's been eaten; alcohol's found its way into a number of the soft-drinks cans. It's like a United Nations of the Homeless: all those different languages, but there's a bond between them. They may not understand the words, but they comprehend the eyes and the gestures. Domino had told him: our eyes betray us. You select your mark by how they look at you. If they're gullible, you'll know; if they want to believe, you'll know. Pick one of them, and the trick's already halfway won.

'And now, onto the stage, please welcome the Amazing Lion!'

Tiger doesn't mind that the announcer has mucked up his name. Actually, it seems fitting. He's thinking of Lafayette's tormented beast. As Tiger walks onstage, he imagines himself in the Empire Theatre, 9 May, 1911. The audience are dressed in their best suits and frocks, ready to be entertained. He's just come from his suite at the Caledonian Hotel, having fed on lobster and champagne. He's sad about his dog, but the show must go on.

'Thank you very much, ladies and gentlemen.' He has taken the microphone from the announcer. There's a bit of feedback and echo from the loudspeaker, but he ignores it. The crowd are still restless. Tiger fixes the mic to its stand, flexes his right hand and produces a perfectly fanned set of playing-cards. There are a few claps and whistles. He makes the deck vanish again. A juggling-ball appears in its place. He seems surprised by this and reaches into his pocket for another. He steps off the stage and approaches the front row. He's already spotted his mark, reaches behind the man's ear and produces the third ball. He's gaining the audience's attention now. Back up onstage, he starts juggling, alternating between all three balls and just two. When juggling two, he uses one hand only. This was actually harder to learn than three. He makes a show of dropping a ball. More applause and whistling.

'Don't clap till I get it right!'

And he does, with even more dexterity. The mark in the front row is on his feet in appreciation. But now the balls are disappearing, leaving Tiger's hands empty. He stands at the front of the stage and takes a bow, then clicks his fingers. The curtain behind him rises, and the box is wheeled onto the stage. The curtain falls again, but Tiger goes behind it, returning with half a dozen swords. He keeps hold of a pair of them, clanking them against one another. Back into the audience so he can hand them over. When the chosen recipients begin to draw sparks from their brief duel, he takes them back. Everyone knows now: the swords are real.

And if real, then the danger also must be real.

Now to select his volunteer. Plenty of arms go up, and Tiger makes a show of long consideration. But there can be only one winner.

Arkady.

Seated just where Tiger had told him to be: second row back on the aisle. Tiger asks for applause as the Russian bounds onto the stage. Tiger opens the vertical box. It's a tight fit for Arkady. Tiger slaps the sides and back, making sure they all know it is solid. Then he gestures for Arkady to squeeze himself in. And closes the door on him, hooking it shut top and bottom. Now he points to two more members of the audience, gestures for them to join him.

'You see, ladies and gentlemen,' he says into the mic, 'it would be too easy for me to do this trick. That's why

you're going to help me. You could say you're my appren-
tices.' Not that the two men know what he's saying. But
he hands them the swords. Then thinks of something and
reaches into his pocket. He's not wearing any special
clothes, just his usual denim jacket and black baggy jeans.
The jacket has been adapted, but not so anyone would
ever notice. He brings a half-eaten chocolate éclair out.

'Is this yours, sir?' Gesturing with it towards the mark
in the front row, who looks down at his lap, realising for
the first time that his precious cake is missing. He rises
to his feet, laughing and clapping. Takes the éclair back
and relishes a large bite from it, while the audience cheer.

Time having passed, Tiger is back at the box. He has
walked all around it, kicking at it with his trainers. Now
he tells the men to run it through with their swords. They
look uncomprehending, so he mimes the act of lunging.
One of them gets the idea and attacks the side of the
box. Then the man on the other side does the same thing.
Tiger holds up his hands in horror.

'Not till I give the signal! There's a special signal or
the magic doesn't work!' He presses his ear to the box.
'You okay in there?'

The audience have grown quiet. They can't help but
hear the soft moan. Tiger looks at them and shakes his
head slowly. The lights have been lowered in the hall; two
spots picking out the stage. There's someone standing by
the far door, arms folded. Almost looks like John Domino,
but Tiger knows it can't be. 'If you want a job doing . . .'
he tells the crowd impatiently. Then he takes the remaining
swords and plunges them into the wood. Gestures for the
two audience members to pull them out again. Sends

them back to their seats with a round of applause. Walks to the box and taps it.

No response.

Looks to the audience, his eyebrows raised. The figure by the far door has vanished. Tries tapping again.

No response.

Quickly, with panicked hands, he fumbles at the catches. Throws the door wide open and stands back.

Because the box is empty. He looks inside, steps inside, steps out again. The crowd whistles and cheers. Tiger slams shut the box and takes his bow.

At the show's end, the Scotland coach comes behind the curtain.

'Pretty nifty,' he says, studying the gashes in the wood. 'The holes are already cut, right? The person in the box knows if they twist their body a certain way, the blades will miss them.'

'Reckon that's how it's done?'

The coach winks. 'I watched one of those shows on TV, they showed you the tricks. Nice touch though . . .'

'What?' Someone else pats Tiger on the back.

'That was magic, by the way,' they say. Tiger recognises one of his team-mates. The room is readying for the DJ. The music's already playing. Gorillaz.

'Getting the Russian to go in the box,' the coach explains. 'Bit of animosity between you on the field . . . made it seem scarier, I suppose.' The coach nods to himself. 'So when's he planned to make the big entrance? Waiting till the dancing's in full swing, eh? Gonnae have him burst out of a cake or something?'

'How d'you mean?'

The coach looks at Tiger, smiles uncomfortably. 'Well, it's not the whole trick, is it? The person in the box has to come back.'

'It's in the rules and regulations, is it?' Tiger asks.

'Come on, Tiger.' The smile downright queasy now. 'Where is he?' The coach makes to check the back wall of the box, but Tiger slaps his arm away.

'My property. No interfering.'

'Where is he?'

'Magic Circle says I can't give away trade secrets.'

The coach sucks in air, jabs a finger into Tiger's chest. 'If you've done what I think you've . . .'

He breaks off as the Russian coach and two of Arkady's team-mates arrive. They shake Tiger's boss's hand, want to shake Tiger's, too. They slap the box and nod and laugh. Then one of them asks a question in Russian, to which Tiger just shrugs. They ask it again, and he shrugs again, opening his arms this time for effect. One of the organisers is called over, and he shouts for the interpreter to join them. There's a huddle around Tiger now and he knows it will grow.

Which is all a magician can ever ask for: to be known; to cause a stir; to be remembered. Tiger reckons Lafayette himself would almost be proud.

Murrayfield
(you're having a laugh)

IRVINE WELSH

I

It was a glorious hot summer's day. Doreen Gow was chopping up spring onions as the tiger nosed into the kitchen. She was aware of its mass from the corner of her weeping eye but at first thought that it was Ross, the neighbour's large crossbreed dog, who often came in when she was cooking.

– I've nothing for ye pal, she began, then she turned and faced the animal. It stopped about a foot away from her and looked straight at her, almost petulant in its regard. It had blood staining the white fur around its bottom jaw. Doreen turned back to the chopping board, felt the knife in her grip. Considered the futility of it and just shut her eyes and waited for her life to end. For some reason she thought of her ex-husband Calum, who'd walked out on her two years ago. She wondered how he'd react when he learned she'd been mauled to death by a tiger. Then an almost silent prayer came into her head in an insistent whisper: as if somebody else was saying it on her behalf. The big cat, after a cursory sniff at the back of her bare leg, turned away and ambled back out through the kitchen door.

Doreen had felt its hot breath on the skin at the back of her knees, then heard the pads on its feet bomp and its claws click across the tiled kitchen floor. It sounded like a dog, rather than a cat. Was she seeing things, hallucinating in the heat? No, she turned around to watch the tiger's hackles moving up slowly, languidly as it exited the room. Doreen followed almost robotically, like she was a crude mechanical device created to simulate the tiger's ambling stride, and pushed the sliding door shut. From behind its frosted glass she could see the outline of the animal as it bounded up the stairs. It seemed as if her hall carpet was ripping under its claws.

That tiger needs tae get its claws cut, she thought. That's terrible, my good carpet.

Doreen looked out the back window towards her well-stocked patio garden. It wasn't the biggest in the neighbourhood, but she kept it tidy with various shrubs, potted plants and climbing roses. It was a balmy, hazy day and she struggled to focus in the shimmering light. She noted that her garden shed needed a new coat of creosote. On the yellow-green lawn next door she saw a familiar brown mound, but it was streaked with blood and completely motionless. The tiger had got Ross, and she hadn't heard a thing. Doreen picked up the phone book and dialled Edinburgh Zoo. A girl's voice came on the other end of the line.

– Edinburgh Zoo-hoo . . .

– Do youse have a tiger that's escaped? Cause I've got one here, Doreen said, lighting up a cigarette. She'd stopped for a few months but had put on too much weight as a result. The Benson & Hedges diet was the only thing that helped; only a cigarette could stop her pigging out on snacks. Thank god that tiger had just feasted on Ross and had a full belly, otherwise it might have gone for her.

– We'll just check, the girl on reception said.

Doreen waited by the phone for a couple of minutes before the girl came back on.

IRVINE WELSH

– I'm really sorry, but I'm no sure who tae ask, the lassie told her.

– Aw.

– It's jist thit ah've only started this week n Gillian's away oan her lunch brek n Yvonne's oaf ill. It's jist thit ah wis telt no tae leave the office here, the receptionist explained. – Mibbee Mr McGinlay would ken but he's no due back till later this afternoon.

– Aw.

– Ah ken yi'll think ah'm daft . . .

It was obviously the young lassie's first job. It's no really fair tae burden a kid with this, Doreen considered.

– Dinnae worry aboot that hen, Doreen reassured the young girl, ah'll jist call the polis.

– Aye, n ah'll ask aroond here, the girl said. Doreen left her number, then hung up. She went to dial the police, then thought twice, remembering when she was with her friend Rena at Jenners, and they met this guy in Princes Street handing out pamphlets. One had informed her that there were only 400 Bengal tigers left in the wild and Doreen worried about the police recklessly shooting the animal, just as they had shot an innocent man a wee while back, down in Suffolk or was it Sussex? Anyway, that blind chap, used to be the Home Secretary, he had condemned them. Condemned them for their lack of vision, Doreen thought with a nervous mischief, her sides slowly shaking in tense laughter. But what would the police do to the animal? No quarter would be given. And there might be no need. That Ross, well, he might have had a go, provoked the tiger.

And it was a majestic beast right enough.

No, instead she called Rena, first at her home where

she got the answerphone, then on her mobile. Her friend immediately confirmed her own instincts, saying that Doreen should keep the police out of it, try the zoo again and ask to speak to somebody in charge. She was indignant about it, but then Rena was a real animal lover.

– I'll be round later, it's only that I'm at Samantha's now and I'm just about to go under the dryer.

Again, Doreen thought. No bad for lady muck. Mind you, it was probably a corrective measure as they'd made a mess of it the other week. Not that Doreen had said as much to Rena cause she'd at least professed to be happy with it, but that lassie never suited a fringe. Never in a million years.

2

Like many postmen of his generation, Malcolm Forbes, a tall, gangly man with long but thinning frizzy blond hair and big, bulging eyes, was a bit of a stoner. Malcolm knew that he shouldn't be having a blow on the job but, fuck it, it was a beautiful, baking hot day and he was down the disused railway line, now a cycle path, well away from prying eyes as he skinned up a big joint of temple ball. The mailbag was heavy and his light-blue post office issue shirt was dark with sweat under his armpits and down his back.

Fuck it, you needed a break.

By the time Malcolm emerged from the banked path, and the camouflage of trees and shrubbery, and stumbled onto the street, he was pretty stoned. Sauntering down the road with his bag now feeling considerably lighter, he only snapped out of his trance when he realised that he was at Mrs Jardine's house. A shudder of caution shook him through his haze. That dug Ross didn't seem to be around; it had bit him once before. He gingerly turned down the garden path and stuck a couple of letters through the box.

Emboldened by the dope and the lack of canine presence Malcolm decided that his tormentor was either out or, better still, tied up to the back post. If so, he'd wind the bastard up. He tiptoed down the side lane to the back in order to check.

When he got round to the back garden, the first thing he saw was a big tiger. It must have been about seven feet long. It was lying on its side on the lawn, reclining in the sun.

– Wow, Malcolm said. He looked at the mangled and chewed corpse beside it. It had got Ross. Ross was a big dog, a crossbreed, but evidently no match for the huge cat. Was a tiger really a cat as such? Malcolm doubted it. He'd once owned a cat, Squeedgie. Squeedgie the Weedgie, he'd called it, as he'd bought it from that Glaswegian window-cleaner boy who drank in the Roseburn Bar. But Squeedgie was nowt like this thing. Anyway, however you looked at it, Ross had got his.

– Wow, Malcolm said again, turning slowly and beating a retreat down the path by the side of the house. As he was going out the front gate, still looking cautiously behind him, Mrs Jardine was approaching. He turned to face her small, frail figure. Despite the intense heat she wore a substantial jacket and her face was pinched as if she was cold.

– Hello son, any post?

– Just stuck a couple of things through the door, Malcolm said, his mouth hanging open in a smile, strangely reminding Mrs Jardine of Ross. She'd got a nice bone from Mr Hall the butcher at Roseburn. She was surprised that Ross wasn't barking, he could usually smell something like this a mile away.

– Only I'm expecting an invitation to my friend's golden wedding anniversary, she informed him, beaming a little. Mrs Jardine was excited at the prospect of getting together with some of her old acquaintances.

– That's nice . . . is that, like, twenty years or what? Malcolm asked.

Mrs Jardine laughed at him. – No son, no, not at all, it's fifty!

Malcolm nodded thoughtfully. – A long time tae be married like, he told her. Fuck me, he'd been married for fifteen months and that was long enough!

– It is that, Mrs Jardine conceded, thinking sadly that it would have been better if she had had a wee bit more time with Crawford. Still, he'd drooled, pished the bed and talked so much shite at the end, his eventual demise came as a relief. It was sad, but on balance the two years of dementia stuck in her head more than the near forty years of marital bliss. Such melancholy thoughts, she pondered. Maybe it was just the age she was at. Still, at least she had Ross.

– Oh, Malcolm said, his thoughts hazy and disconnected, that temple ball was some smoke right enough! – I nearly forgot! Maybe you'd better watch. There's a tiger in the back gairden. Unfortunately it got Ross.

– What do you mean, it got Ross? What are you on about laddie, Mrs Jardine half-laughed.

– Eh . . . Malcolm hesitated. They were trying to sack you for anything these days. He wasn't trained as a bereavement counsellor or anything like that. Aye, they were just waiting to trip you up. Wee Russell, nice wee guy, caught on CCTV doing a bit of shouting at the football and they'd sacked him for being a hooligan. No, he'd said enough already. – I'm no really sure, but the best thing to do might be tae phone the mail people. At the depot likes.

– But . . . but . . . Mrs Jardine stammered incomprehensibly and irritably – Ah cannae see how the mail affects Ross. What's aw this aboot a tiger? Yir daft laddie, jist plain daft!

– I have to go, Malcolm said, departing with haste.

That boy was on drugs, Mrs Jardine thought. It's no good, not at all. She wasn't going to clipe on the laddie, not with jobs being what they were, but maybe she would write to *The Scotsman*, just to make a general point. The post was obviously going the same way as the railways. It had taken her daughter Elisabeth eight hours to get up by train from London the other week. The rot had to be stopped. This drugs business worried her. It was even here now, in Murrayfield. The world was going crazy. They were even talking about having football here now, at the rugby stadium! The rugby crowd itself was bad enough these days, far removed from the gentlemen of old. And now we were being expected to put up with casual yobs every other week, and even worse, Glaswegians coming through. That meant foul language, bottles of cheap wine and public urination on the streets and in the gardens.

That was bad enough, but the drugs were worse. They seemed to get everywhere. It was probably thanks to the likes of that nyaff across the back, he'd bought his house – a lovely big house – on drugs money. You could tell; the tattoos, the jewellery, the fancy clothes and big car. And all those noisy people who came round. The language. And it was like a fortress since he'd built that big wall, you couldn't even see into his garden now. A house of ill-repute if ever there was. Oh aye, he was nice enough at first, always let on, said 'good morning'. But then he was shown in his true colours, cursing and swearing when Ross bested his pit bull. An ugly, nasty thing it was, but Ross saw it off. Aye, he didnae half!

Then the pit bull had gone and attacked a lassie from the school and had been put down. It wasn't the animal's fault of course: they were only as good or as bad as their owners. Aye, it was the likes of that nyaff from the council scheme who should be put down, Mrs Jardine thought with some satisfaction. That would teach them to look after their pets!

But it was funny that Ross wasn't making a fuss, he must have heard her coming back.

– Rossy . . . Rossy . . . As she went round the back of the house, Mrs Jardine screamed in horror as she saw the remains of her dog. He had been torn to shreds. She couldn't believe it. What was it that bloody post fool had said about a tiger? She looked around but there was no sign of any damn tiger or anything else.

– Ross . . . she sobbed. That bastard, that monster on the post! The drugs had got to him, warped his brain and he'd destroyed Ross in a frenzied attack. Aye, he'd

IRVINE WELSH

complained about Ross before, and this was the result of his twisted anger! Mrs Jardine hobbled into the house and called the Post Office.

– Tore your dog apart, you say? the depot supervisor Bill Niven scoffed. – Our Malcolm? Come on missus. That laddie wouldnae hurt a fly.

– But . . . but . . . but . . . Mrs Jardine sputtered.

The door went and she slammed the phone down. She went through to answer it and it was Doreen Gow from next door, in a state of some panic.

– Can I come in? Doreen asked.

– Well, it's no a good time, Mrs Jardine sobbed. – It's Ross . . .

– The tiger got him, Doreen squealed, it's oot here. I need tae come in! And she pushed past Mrs Jardine and slammed the door shut. Mrs Jardine was affronted. This woman was evidently as crazed as that murdering postie bastard, perhaps even more. She had always regarded Doreen as a flighty one with a wanton streak, but she'd never expected anything like this from her. It just went to show.

– Did . . . did thon postman laddie gie you anything? Mrs Jardine enquired of Doreen. Aye, the bloody harlot was obviously demented on drugs.

Doreen looked wildly at her. There *was* the package from Tupperware.

– He brought me something, she said.

Mrs Jardine looked at the woman in disgust.

– And you just took it, she spat.

– Aye. Aye ah did, Doreen said, wondering what was wrong with her neighbour. The old bitch is going senile, she thought.

Mrs Jardine looked harshly at her. This harlot was as bold as brass. Parties, noise, no wonder her husband had gone. She'd obviously been at it with thon postman. Maybe poor Ross had disturbed their drug-fuelled orgy and they'd spitefully poisoned him and in deranged bloodlust had carved him up, torn him apart with power tools. Mrs Jardine glanced out the back window into Doreen's garden. The door on her shed was open!

The old woman looked harshly at her neighbour and took a step backwards.

– Look, Doreen tried to explain, there was a tiger. It escaped from the zoo, I think. It got Ross. Sorry.

– Ah know he's gone, Mrs Jardine sobbed, before turning on Doreen. – Aye, and it suits you doesn't it? It bloody well suits you awright.

– What dae ye mean?

– Bloody tiger nonsense. You and thon postie. Youse never liked that dog, Mrs Jardine tearfully accused.

– I fed him, Doreen retorted in a grating righteousness. – Don't tell me that I never liked Ross. I fed Ross.

Her indignation was impacting on Mrs Jardine, who was starting to feel that neither Doreen nor Malcolm had killed Ross. The fight was leaving her. – But if there was an escaped tiger, you never raised the alarm. Ye let my Ross die!

Doreen bristled again, her hands on her hips. – For your information, Ross was finished off by the time I saw what happened. And I did try to help, I phoned the zoo straight away, she said; then, noticing Mrs Jardine's pain, she adopted a more conciliatory stance and tone. – A nice lassie said she'd phone back.

– Aw aye, aw aye . . . and what did she say?

Doreen looked at her in guilty silence. Eventually she was moved to confess. – Well, she told me tae call the police. But I never. Well, what do they know?

It was true, Mrs Jardine considered bitterly. The police had gone like the railways, like the post. There was a time when you at least knew where you stood with them, even if they weren't that good. Now it had all changed. There was even a top policeman down in London who was one of those funny fellows who loved other men and he was encouraging the blacks to smoke drugs. No wonder there was so much rape. No wonder criminals like him across the back were strutting around like peacocks when you had a bunch of Jessies in charge of policing!

Doreen was thinking about Ross, who could be a contrary beast. – Anywey, mibbe Ross wis tae blame, she said, – ah mean, he must have had a go at thon big cat. It wis bound tae be feelin isolated n hunted. The last thing it needed wis a dug huvin a go!

The outraged old woman snapped back at Doreen. Who was she, this drunken slut, her that had brought men back at the weekend. – You don't know what yir talkin about! Ross was tied up! Ross couldnae help it. Eh couldnae run. Eh wis mauled. Mauled tae death!

Doreen was having none of it. – Aye, n whae left the dug tied up? Eh? Eh? Answer me that? Who left poor Ross helpless? Eh?

The words thudded like arrows into Mrs Jardine's chest. She looked out her window and then she saw the tiger. It was pishing against her rosebushes. – There it is! There's the bloody killer!

– Magnificent lookin animal but, Doreen said with respect as she glanced over her neighbour's shoulder. Mrs Jardine, though, was still staring out at the beast. Something seemed to cross over in her. That thing had killed her Ross and it was just lying there, desecrating his corpse: devouring it at its leisure. The spoiled body of her poor dog, the tiger had opened it up, dragged its entrails out. Before Doreen could stop her, Mrs Jardine had gone to a cupboard, picked up a broom and opened the patio door. She charged outside, screaming at the beast, – You kilt Ross! You kilt Ross, ya bloody bugger!

The tiger buckled back on its hunkers, and let out a low growl at the woman. Then it suddenly leapt, flaying Mrs Jardine in one rip across the face and neck. Doreen slammed the patio doors shut.

At least she's wi Ross and Crawford now, her neighbour thought, as she watched the beast tear at the prostrate, twitching body.

Well, soon.

Trembling with fear and deeply confused, Doreen found her neighbour's drinks cabinet. There was only whisky. She poured a glass and took a big swallow, almost gagging on its burning sourness. The second one was better. Then she phoned the zoo, recognising the voice of the same girl on the line. – Wis it you that ah phoned earlier?

The girl seemed to register her. – Aw . . . you're that woman, eh.

– Aye.

There was a pause for a few seconds on the line.

Doreen grew impatient. – Well, that tiger, huv you goat um?

– Eh, ah'm no really sure likes, the girl admitted, what aboot your one, is he still loose?

– He's here . . . it's dangerous . . . it's awfay, she said, looking out the window. Mrs Jardine's corpse lay a few feet away from Ross's. The tiger seemed to have gone. No, it was lying in the shade by the garden shed.

– Ye'd better gie's the address, the girl ventured, then with sudden relief said, – naw, speak tae Gillian, that's her jist walked in the now.

There was another pause on the line. – Hello, Gillian Forest here. Are you the lady with the tiger?

– Aye, but it's nothing tae dae wi me. It just came into ma house. It's next door it really affects.

– Which one is it, Khan or Lady?

– Whit dae ye mean?

– Well, it's, eh, like Khan's a laddie and Lady's a lassie.

Doreen was nonplussed at this. She had no experience in sexing tigers. When she and Calum got married they'd had a cat, Sally, but that was a long time ago and it was hard to tell from here. It was distressing though, to watch the animal gnawing at Mrs Jardine. It had pulled her thin body into the shade. – How kin youse no check?

– What?

– How kin youse no check?

– Well, Mr Turnbull that normally looks after the tigers is on holiday and Davey's been off sick. We've definitely got one here but the other one might be gone. But we're no certain cause it might be hidin in the concrete enclosure. Ye cannae really see in right. And both the men that work with them aren't in today. There's naebody that's qualified tae go intae the enclosure, see. Ah took a look and I think it's Lady that might have gone. She can be a bugger. Somebody did say that cage door wis open the other night, Gillian explained.

– But how's that?

There was a pause before Gillian sheepishly admitted, – Somebody forgot tae lock it right.

– Well, ah'll huv ye know that it got Ross and Mrs Jardine.

– Is Ross the cougar?

– What?

– Ross, is he the cougar?

– Aw, naw, Ross is the dug. Looks like a Doberman but he's actually a cross between a German Shepherd and a Rottweiler. Or ah think eh is . . . or was.

– Aw! Gillian exclaimed, suddenly relieved. – That wis ootside then, ootside ay the zoo!

– Aye.

Satisfied now, Gillian said, – Disnae really affect us if it aw happened ootside. Sorry. Ah dinnae ken what tae suggest . . . the police maybe.

– Aw, right, Doreen said, – cheerio then. She put the phone back down on the cradle. She supposed that the lassie had a point.

3

Goagsie Landles and his girlfriend Mona McGovern had just returned from Texas, one of their favourite holiday jaunts. They had been stopped at airport customs in the

Green Channel, the only ones who were apprehended in this manner and had had their luggage meticulously searched. Goagsie was charged duty on a second pair of cowboy boots he had packed away, though thankfully not on the ones he had on nor on the Stetson he was wearing.

Welcome hame, right enough, Goagsie thought bitterly.

That would be the one, a big ranch out in Texas. The big country, right enough: freedom from interference and disapproval. No wonder that Bush cunt had a ranch there. If you were Scottish, you were well in back there in the American South. A place where a proper Scottish accent carried weight, no like here in Murrayfield where the snobby, bools-in-the-mooth bastards looked down on you every time you opened your gob.

When they looked at Goagsie, all they saw was the shorn hair and the tattoos. He knew what they were thinking, that this house (biggest in the fuckin street by the way) was bought with cocaine money. Which, granted, was true, but that was his business. Luckily, he had a huge garden and had Billy coming in to feed the tiger in the large enclosure he'd built. He always worried that the authorities would be tipped off, maybe by that nosy old fucker across the back, in those smaller houses, that Mrs Jardine. She was always trying tae peer over the wall. Nosy auld trout.

Texas. The Lone Star State. Yes, sir, they'd said to Goagsie in the bars and restaurants of San Antonio and Austin. Nae difference between a Pilton buck and a Murrayfield yin oot thair. Aye, you could sell a house like his and buy a decent-sized ranch and ye'd still have change for a stable

ay poxy wee hoors. And have a steak the size ay a surf-
board on yir plate every day!

Aye, fuck Britain, and fuck Scotland, he thought. Fucking shitehoose full of losers. But, he lamented ruefully,
he had made mistakes as well. When he had parties
Goagsie couldn't resist showing off Kipling to the boys.
But sometimes they had dopey tarts along, not lassies
who knew the score but ten-a-penny daft party chicks
they'd picked up en route from some nightclub, usually
Ronnie's place. Gabby as fuck, some people: you never
kent who tae trust. Aye, always a problem. And fuckin
Mona here . . .

He watched his girlfriend walk on ahead, pushing her
trolley through the airport in her high heels, clad in a
tight silver designer tracksuit with platinum highlights in
her blonde hair. Nippy as fuck as she never got to work
on her tan the second week cause the food poisoning
she'd picked up at the seafood place had made her ill. It
was her who wanted to go into that minging Mexican
joint. Authentic, she'd called it. It was authentically minging and the silly cow didn't know which end to turn to
the toilet all week.

Goagsie hated the indignity of getting a taxi, but he
was barred from driving. They loaded up the luggage and,
as they were getting into the cab, Mona went over on
her heels, one of them clinically snapping off. – Aw for
fuck's sake! she spat.

They were the Gucci ones that she liked, but Goagsie
felt a surge of vindication as he had told her repeatedly
about the idiocy of wearing high heels while travelling.
He said nothing but his crocodile grin spoke volumes.

– What? Mona asked, rolling down the window and spitting out her chewing gum.

Goagsie relaxed back into his seat, pulled the Stetson over his eyes. – Looks like we brought some Texan weather with us, he mused contentedly.

He was looking forward to seeing Kipling again. It was the first time they'd been separated in the eight months he'd owned the tiger; purchased from a Romanian circus touring Britain. Fifteen grand. The boy had offered to chuck in a bride for another three grand, had even shown Goagsie a book of pictures, the lot. And he was more tempted than he let on. Eastern Europeans would be lighter on fuel and maintenance than the likes of Mona. Naw, the mystic Far East was his future though, next time he needed new fanny he was going Thai.

At least George Turnbull, the keeper of the big cats at Edinburgh Zoo, had been helpful with the care of Kipling. A good lad, George: educated, but not all up himself like some of them. Shame about the ching problem. Still, that was his business. Or his and Goagsie's.

The vehicle romped along in the taxi lane into the outskirts of the city, through Corstorphine and into Murray-field, turning into Goagsie's driveway and scrunching down the gravel path to a halt outside his front door. Goagsie pulled out the luggage and paid the driver. Mona was still sour as fuck, making a big show of hopping to the door of the house.

Fuckin high heels oan a plane . . . she's huvin a fuckin laugh.

He opened the door of his home and stuck the cases inside. He shouted, – Billy! But there was no sign of the fucker, he who was meant to be Kipling-sitting and house-watching. An acrid bile of rage rose from Goagsie's gut, leaving a metallic taste in his mouth and forcing him to swallow hard. That unreliable cunt had probably taken off on the pish and neglected poor Kipling. Or maybe the dozy wee twat was holed up wi some daft bit ay fanny somewhere.

See if that cunt's starved ma Kipling . . .

Goagsie went through the house and outside to the compound where he kept the tiger secured, and the first thing he saw was the open gate of the cage.

Aw naw . . .

A thousand images of Billy burned in his head, most of which involved him, a blowtorch and a set of power tools. Then, when he stepped out, he was assaulted by a pervasive stink in his nostrils and throat, and he wretched violently. Somebody had got there first. There was a shapeless form on the ground. He could make out a ragged, ripped Heart of Midlothian away football strip. Mixed through it was a collection of bones. A large pool of blood had dried in the sun. Goagsie stepped closer and contemplated a torn-faced skull, with both the eyes still in it, looking up at him, frozen in death into an expression of dumb fear. Bluebottles buzzed and danced around the corpse, flying in and out of its mouth and ears.

Goagsie booted the head as hard as he could, wrenching it from its flimsy, near-severed attachment at the neck. It smashed against the compound wall with force, rolling on a little before coming to rest with the eyes looking up at him again. – You're fuckin lucky Kipling goat tae ye first ya cunt! Ah widnae huv been that easy oan ye!

He stomped on the head repeatedly, until it started to crush under the heels of his cowboy boots.

Mona came outside, witnessed the carnage and started screaming: – What huv ye done tae Billy!

– It wisnae me, it wis Kipling, the daft cunt let Kipling oot!

Mona gasped in horror: – You . . . you're tae blame for this, Goagsie!

Goagsie looked pointedly at her. – Ah've telt ye before, ah dinnae like the word 'blame'.

– Ye never fuckin well do when it's attached tae you. You're horrible, Goagsie, you've nae decency, nae remorse fir poor Billy even!

– That fuckin spazwit? Goagsie pointed at the strewn, defiled corpse, for the head that lay mashed next to it was no longer identifiable as Billy. – Simpleton wisnae right in the heid, wanderin aroond in that replica fitba shirt wi that daft New York Yankees hat oan like a fuckin community care case. He was a fuckin vegetable. Ah'm surprised Kipling could be bothered eating the bastard. It's natural fuckin selection: Kipling is a top-ay-the-food-chain predator and aw he wis daein wis helpin the natural order ay things by keepin prey populations like that bam Billy in check.

– Billy was meant tae be your friend!

– Billy worked for me. He got fucking careless, couldnae dae a simple task. Kipling made him pay for his mistake, the drug-dealer said, suddenly misty-eyed in admiration. – Took the cunt oot good style but eh?

– Well, you'll go doon for it, Goagsie. Ah'm tellin ye,

you'll dae time fir that fuckin tiger n it'll serve ye right, Mona said, heading back inside.

– Aye, right, Goagsie spat. She was giving it the big one but she knew which side her bread was buttered on too much to grass him up. But that fucking phantom Billy: now he had a chewed-up corpse to dispose of. You asked some folk to do a simple task. Just one fucking simple task. But naw. Now poor Kipling would probably be in the hands of the authorities, or even dead, shot down callously by some dickhead polisman all flushed with the excitement of being allowed to use a shooter and thinking he's some fucking SWAT team expert. They'd made him get poor Tyson put down. It was because that daft wee lassie was wearing the silly hat – that always freaked Tyson out. He was determined that he wasn't going to lose Kipling, his 430-pound five-year-old male Bengal tiger. Not after what he'd paid for him and all the expenses he'd shelled out on the animal's keep.

Goagsie desperately combed the back garden, but there were few traces of Kipling, and it was difficult to work out where he'd gone. After a while though, it dawned on him that there was only one way the tiger could have got out – over the wall. If he'd climbed onto the shed roof, he could have leapt from there onto the roof of the compound, then onto the adjoining wall and over into one of the gardens in the small bungalows behind Goagsie's large villa.

Catching the whiff of tiger excrement, he found himself paraphrasing an old poem:

Tiger, tiger burning bright
In your cage that smells of shite

But Kipling wasn't in the cage. However, maybe it was a while ago that he'd killed Billy, then perhaps noshed back what he could of the unpalatable little bastard before heading off. Maybe he'd only left the garden recently. If so, there might be a chance to get him before the polis or those fuckwits from the council got involved!

As Goagsie strode out, he met Malcolm the postman in his driveway. – Eh, Mr Landles?

– Aye . . .

– Goat something here for ye. Ye huv tae sign fir it. Recorded delivery.

– Fuck . . . Goagsie gasped. He was in a hurry; he didn't need this now. He felt his jaw pulling in an involuntary yawn as if a stranger whose fist was wrapped in cotton wool had just hit him. It was the jetlag kicking in and he had to find Kipling. He grabbed the pen from the postman and signed in the boxes, chucking the package onto his doorstep.

Malcolm was about to remonstrate that he had signed his name in both boxes, when he was supposed to print it in one, but he knew that Goagsie Landles was a known face and worried that it might be taken the wrong way. He had a stoned thought following on from 'don't take this the wrong way' and smirked as he considered Goagsie Landles and the tiger in a bout of rough sex. In his vision the tiger had a striped orange and black cock and Goagsie was getting it up him . . . a tiger tadger . . . 'Don't take this the wrong way' played on a loop in his brain and he started sniggering.

– You takin the fuckin pish mate? Goagsie challenged, his gangster paranoia kicking in big time.

Aw fuck, I've goat myself intae deep shite now, Malcolm thought. He believed in the theory that people took drugs to make them more of what they already were. That was gangsters for you: as paranoid as fuck to start with, so they probably only took cocaine as a way of justifying feeling so anxious. – Eh, ah'm jist a bit nervous and freaked out man, there's a big tiger on the loose.

Goagsie's eyes bulged out as if on sticks. – Show me where? he demanded, pushing the gangly postman down the path.

– Kipling! Kippers! Ma wee laddie!

They headed out and down the street, and round to Mrs Jardine's house, Malcolm, with his heavy bag, struggling to match the purposeful strides of the brawny, tattooed drug baron. When they got to Mrs Jardine's front door the postie refused to go any further. – You're on your own now man, he said.

– Dinnae phone the polis, right? Goagsie threatened. For a few brief seconds he entertained the notion of adding 'ya cunt' to the sentence, but decided against it.

– No way man, Malcolm said, stepping back. – I'm out of here, it's not my business.

– That's right mate, Goagsie nodded sternly, then winked at the departing postman, – I'll see ye awright later on.

He ventured slowly down the side of the house into the back garden. He could only see two corpses, that of Mrs Jardine and her crazy dug. Then he heard a tapping on glass and turned to see Doreen on the other side of the patio doors, frantically signalling at him. She pointed across the lawn behind him and he jumped round to see Kipling sitting in the shade.

On seeing Goagsie the huge beast rose and moved towards his would-be master. After tasting Billy's salty flesh, the tough dogmeat and the stringy, meagre snack that was Mrs Jardine had failed to satisfy the hungry creature.

Goagsie approached as the beast moved into a crouching position. – Kippers . . . Kippers . . . down boy . . .

The tiger sprang forward, going for the chunky, six-foot-three hoodlum's throat. Outraged, the gangster instinctively tried to ram the nut on the beast, but only succeeded in jamming his entire head in its open jaws. Its fangs ripped through the Stetson and drove into his skull, and the tiger's big claws flayed at Goagsie, who was hammering piston-like kidney-punches into the animal's flanks. One strong right hook snapped one of the big cat's ribs.

Doreen was watching in shock with Rena, who had come in through the front door. – Maybe we should get the police after all, Rena said, as man and beast remain locked in combat. But the tiger was choking; waves of bile were surging up from its stomach but were stopped from being expelled by Goagsie's head and the rim of the Stetson, which was wedged in the big cat's gullet. The beast tried to crush the thug's skull in its powerful jaws, but Goagsie's bullet-cranium held firm and the animal slowly choked, falling over and taking the still-trapped outlaw down with him.

Although the tiger was only semi-conscious and very weak by the time they arrived, the police marksmen decided to take no chances and despatched five bullets into him. Firemen then had to lever the dead cat's jaws apart in order to free Goagsie's head.

Goagsie survived, but due to the head injuries sustained in the tiger's attack he was never the same again. Compensation-seeking relatives claimed that one of the police bullets had struck him, but this was dismissed after a full medical examination. Old friends would be dismayed as they saw him feeding the ducks at Inverleith pond, drooling and talking to himself. He was lifted for exposing himself to schoolchildren and the arresting officers found themselves surprisingly moved to see the big gangster reduced to tears of frustration. Mona left him for an associate of his, who was heavily involved in the ill-fated Scotland-Ireland joint Euro 2008 bid.

He now has little contact with the outside world, mostly passing time by watching videos and playing computer games. One exception is Doreen who occasionally calls over with some homemade soup in a Tupperware bowl.

AUTHOR BIOGRAPHIES

ALEXANDER McCALL SMITH

Alexander McCall Smith is the author of the six *No. 1 Ladies' Detective Agency* novels. He is the author of numerous other books, including the *44 Scotland Street* and *The Sunday Philosophy Club* series. Before turning to writing full-time, he was Professor of Medical Law at the University of Edinburgh and a member of national and international bodies concerned with bioethics.

In 2004 he was made Author of the Year at the British Book Awards. Other awards include: the Saga Award for Wit, the Dagger in the Library Award of the Crime Writers' Association, and the Walpole Medal for Excellence. This year he was shortlisted for a Quill Award in the United States. His books have been translated into thirty-six languages and have been bestsellers throughout the world.

In his spare time he is a member of an amateur orchestra, the Really Terrible Orchestra (RTO), which he co-founded with his wife, a doctor. He lives in Edinburgh.

IAN RANKIN

Born in Fife in 1960, Ian Rankin graduated from the University of Edinburgh and has since been employed as grape-picker, swineherd, taxman, alcohol researcher, hi-fi journalist and punk musician. His first Rebus novel, *Knots & Crosses*, was published in 1987 and the Rebus books have now been translated into 22 languages. Ian and his wife lived for six years in France in the 1980s and regularly visit there. Awarded the OBE in 2002, Ian Rankin is an elected Hawthornden Fellow, and a past winner of the prestigious Chandler-Fulbright Award, as well as two CWA short-story 'Daggers' and the 1997 CWA Macallan Gold Dagger for Fiction for *Black & Blue*, which was also shortlisted for the Mystery Writers of America 'Edgar' award for best novel. In September 2005 Ian Rankin was awarded *GQ* Writer of the Year. He lives in Edinburgh with his wife and two sons.

J. K. ROWLING

J. K. (Joanne Kathleen) Rowling was born in 1965 and grew up in Chepstow. At Exeter University she earned a French and Classics degree. She worked for a spell in London at Amnesty International and started to outline the plot for the Harry Potter series during a Manchester to London train journey.

After teaching English in Portugal, she moved to Edinburgh, where *Harry Potter & the Philosopher's Stone* was eventually completed in 1996. The following summer the world was introduced to Harry Potter. The six books have been some of the fastest and biggest selling books in history, with the entire series selling 300 million copies worldwide. In November 2005, the fourth Harry Potter film was released.

J. K. Rowling was awarded an OBE for services to children's literature in 2000. She is the President of the

One Parent Families charity, and the Patron of The Multiple Sclerosis Society Scotland.

IRVINE WELSH

Irvine Welsh's debut novel, *Trainspotting*, was adapted into a hugely successful film and stage play. His other books are *The Acid House* (filmed by Paul McGuigan), *Marabou Stork Nightmares*, *Ecstasy: Three Tales of Chemical Romance* (to be filmed by Rob Heydon), *Filth*, *Glue* and *Porno* (a sequel to *Trainspotting*). His new novel, *The Bedroom Secrets of the Master Chefs*, will be out in the summer of 2006. His work has been globally translated. He does occasional journalism, mainly for *The Daily Telegraph* and *The Guardian*, and is a partner in Four Ways Films with Antonia Bird, Mark Cousins and Robert Carlyle. A film, *The Meat Trade*, co-scripted with Dean Cavanagh, is due to be filmed in spring 2006. A new stage play, *Babylon Heights*, also co-written with Dean Cavanagh, will be staged simultaneously in Dublin and San Francisco in 2006. He now lives in Dublin but makes frequent visits home to Edinburgh.

ONECITY TRUST

The OneCity Trust was established as a result of a report commissioned by Edinburgh's Lord Provost in 1998 to discover the extent of social exclusion in the city and, most importantly, what could be done about it.

The OneCity Trust channels funds, enthusiasm and ideas from the individuals and companies to make a positive difference for communities throughout our city by supporting educational and social welfare projects.

OneCity is not simply another grant-awarding charity, we are a conduit for funds and ideas. We don't divert sponsorship from other causes but enhance the support they receive. We are a route through which communities, businesses and individuals can combine their resources to offer sustainable long-term solutions to the social divisions in the city. We are all a part of this process and our aims cannot be achieved without your participation.

OneCity Trust benefits from wide support: the Lord Provost of Edinburgh is our President and our ambassadors are Sir Tom Farmer, Stephen Hendry, Ian Rankin, Irvine Welsh, Gordon Strachan, Baroness Smith, Mrs Unis and Alexander McCall Smith. Our business champions include State Street Corporation, Baillie Gifford and Scottish & Newcastle.

Further information:

OneCity Trust, Scottish Community Foundation,
126 Canongate, Edinburgh EH8 8DD
tel. +44(0)131 524 0300; email info@onecitytrust.org
website www.onecitytrust.org

ACKNOWLEDGEMENTS

As the Chair of the OneCity Trust I would like to extend on its behalf sincere thanks to the Rt Hon. Lesley Hinds, Lord Provost of Edinburgh and President of the Trust, for bringing our authors together and to Alexander McCall Smith, Ian Rankin and Irvine Welsh for their enthusiasm, time and dedication throughout the development of *One City* and to J. K. Rowling for her inspiring introduction.

We would also like to thank our development manager, Teri Wishart, whose management and hard work were essential in bringing *One City* to life, Jan Rutherford from Publicity & the Printed Word for managing to hold things together when it seemed like they might fall apart, Imogen Assenti for supporting and guiding the project with calm assurance, and Polygon editor Alison Rae. Many thanks are also owed to all involved at the Scottish Community Foundation for their support and to Murray Buchanan at Maclay Murray & Spens for making sense of the incomprehensible.

Further thanks to the considerable support of *The Scotsman*, Ottakar's bookstores, Hookson design and all the staff of the Edinburgh Festival Theatre.

Extra special thanks are extended to Neville Moir and Hugh Andrew from Polygon for their patience and good humour.

Hamish Buchan
Chair of the OneCity Trust